MISTER GREY

MISTER GREY

RICHARD WHITE

FOUR WALLS EIGHT WINDOWS

NEW YORK

© 1992 Richard White

Published in the United States by:

Four Walls Eight Windows
PO Box 548
Village Station
New York, New York 10014

First printing May 1992.

Library of Congress Cataloging-in-Publication Data:
White, Richard, 1931—
Mister Grey/Richard White.—1st ed.
p. cm.
ISBN: 0-941423-71-9
I. Title.
PS3573.H47475M57 1991
813'.54—dc20   91-25158
CIP
Text designed by Cindy LaBreacht.
Printed in the United States.

TO MY BROTHERS:

JOHN, DONALD, DAVID,
AND TO THE POET CONNELLAN.
HE IS MY BROTHER, TOO.

ACKNOWLEDGEMENTS:

Thanks are owing to

Fr. Solanus Casey (he knows why);

to Lynne Woodside,

for safe haven when winds are cold;

to Linda Goff, for guarding the archives;

and to the faithful few.

So faithful. So few.

PROLOGUE

I have been a long time away from Wyoming. But there is a part of me that never left. Sometimes, as I walk across the Common of a mild April day, on my way home from tending to the symptoms, aches and wheezes of the Back Bay aristocracy, a playful wind blows in from the west and carries me back in spirit to a time and place so distant now as to seem another world, another age.

I smile to think what Sheriff Finn would make of Charles Prescott, M.D., of Boston and its mannered Brahmins, these narrow streets, prim houses and tame lawns.

And Josiah Grey, would he be pleased to see me now that I am the physician that he himself had longed to be? Would it comfort him to know that I read my Horace and my Vergil still?

I wish I knew what has become of Josiah Grey. I wish I could tell him that time has done its work, that Sukey's grief has long since healed. She no longer tends the flowers on that lonely roadside grave. She queens it in a glittering circle presided over by one of the West's most powerful men in Washington, the man who parlayed the Moncreiff fortune into a brilliant political career.

I'd want him to know that all is well between us, that I have a great kindness for him, and a childish wish to give an account of myself. It would gladden my heart to see him, to let him know I have tried to become the man he saw in the boy I used to be.

Call it an old bachelor's fancy if you like, but I do believe I could rest content just knowing that my life and work had earned an approving smile from Mr. Grey.

CHAPTER I

The last time Father licked me I was twelve years old. It must have made the desired impression, for I cannot recall that I was ever in serious trouble with him again. But then, Father was a man remarkable for his forbearance. I never knew a man who was slower to pass judgment on a fellow creature than Father was. And, really, about the only thing that could light a fire in those mild eyes was when he sniffed out an injustice anywhere in the vicinity. That was why I got thrashed. I'd been unjust.

I knew better, of course. But when Harney Jakes suggested that we tie that calf to the bell rope of the schoolhouse, it seemed harmless enough. How was I to know that Miss Sarah Louise Hathaway would take a fit and run off like the boogerman was after her? Shoot, it wasn't even a very big calf.

But Sheriff Finn came to the house, and he told Father what had happened, and Father went pale and his nostrils pinched in, and I knew the signs. A storm was coming.

I hadn't time to stuff a book down my britches, and it wouldn't have worked anyway. Father was onto all the dodges. He summoned me to the parlor, right in front of the Sheriff, and he said, "Charles, Sheriff Finn has been telling me of a most distressing incident."

When Father called me "Charles," it was not a good sign. I flashed a look at the Sheriff, but he only gave me the fish eye, so I knew I was in for it. Ordinarily, the Sheriff and I were on good terms. I spent a lot of time just loafing around his office, looking at the reward notices and swapping lies. But I could see I was in a bad place, and I knew I would lose my standing with the Sheriff if I was to whine or make excuses. So I said, "What is it, Sir?"

"Some boys tied a poor defenseless animal to the bellrope at the school."

Sheriff Finn took a keen interest in the plaster overhead.

"Do you know anything about that, Charles?"

I swallowed hard. "Yes, Sir. I done it."

"Did it," Father corrected. "Well, you did not do it alone, and you think, I am sure, that taking sole credit for this outrage will spare you your desserts. But you are mistaken. I will thank you to wait for me in your room."

I went. It never occurred to me to run. Father was not a man to run from. He had such command over himself that he inspired a kind of obedience worthy of "Casabianca."

I flung myself across my bed and listened to the rumble of voices below. Father must have known how well I could monitor events taking place downstairs, but he never alluded to it. Indeed, he took advantage of it, as I was to learn years afterward. I can still remember his foxy smile when, the year before his death, I was sitting with him in the parlor reminiscing over the boy I had been.

"I realize now," I had said, "what a difficult task you had, Sir, in raising me without Mother there to help."

"Easiest job I ever had," he said, drawing his shawl a bit more snugly about his thin shoulders. "Whenever I needed to get a particular point across to you, I had only to wait till you had gone on up to bed, and then articulate my position to Clara, or to any caller who happened by, and I knew that you would receive the message as surely as if it had come by Western Union."

I was thirty-two years old when he told me that, but I turned as red and felt about as sheepish as I did on that night of my last whipping.

From my listening post I heard the Sheriff say, "I hope you will not come down too hard on the little feller, Mr. Prescott. It warn't nothin' more'n a prank, same as all boys are bound to try sometime or other."

"Sheriff, I am obliged to you for your concern, and I thank you for letting me know of this," said Father. I could picture him rocking back and forth on his heels as he clutched the lapels of his broadcloth coat. "But cruelty is an abominable trait. I would rather see my son a drunkard or a cardsharp than live to see him grow up cruel."

"Well, I don't believe your boy has ever took a drink—"

"That was by way of example, Sheriff. A bit of hyperbole, perhaps, but no less sincere for that."

I guess "hyperbole" was more than Sheriff Finn was prepared to tackle that day or any other. He left, and Father came up the stairs, razor strop in hand. He did what he believed he had to do, and he did it with that vigor which men of character invariably employ in duties they wish were not theirs to perform.

"Now, Charles," said Father, "I trust you understand why you were punished."

"Yes, Sir," I said, snuffling back my tears and rubbing my smarting behind.

"No gentleman, and certainly no Christian gentleman, ever inflicts wanton cruelty on the weak and the helpless. You may tell more about a man's character from the way he uses his horse or his dog than from his conduct toward his neighbor. A man who dares not kick his neighbor may kick his dog with impunity. And such a man will not scruple to kick you, if he believes that you cannot kick back."

"Yes, Sir."

"Now go to bed, and remember me in your prayers."

"Good night, Father."

Odd, even then I was not angry with Father. I would like to believe that it was because I understood and appreciated his sense of justice. But I was a boy, and my bottom burned, and I was certain as I was of the sunrise that Harney Jakes's father would only laugh when

Sheriff Finn told him, or maybe cuss Harney for not butchering the calf and bringing home the beef.

When I discussed the matter with Clara, she said, "I expect you got just sense enough to know that your pa is the smartest man in the Territory. So it's natural that when he does somethin' or says somethin' you should know it is right.

"I just hope to gracious you gets some more sense soon. Now there ain't no schoolmarm and no school, and you'll be underfoot and into mischief till I'm gone distracted."

Clara's black face wrinkled like a walnut shell as she tried her level best to look fierce. Then the sun broke through, and she smiled wider than all Wyoming. "Land, I never hear such a screechin' as that Miz Hathaway set up. A body would've thought you boys had turned loose a pack of hydrophoby skunks on her."

"I didn't mean for to chase her out of town, Clara," I said. That was the truth. I rather liked Sarah Louise Hathaway for all her old-maidy ways, and despite the fact that she took an obvious shine to Father, which made me sweat some for fear he might do something foolish. But I needn't have worried. I should have known that Father was not likely to be much taken with a lady who was scared of a measly little calf.

It didn't strike me till I had loped halfway through town that April morning that Father had jawed me about the calf, that he had walloped me on account of the calf, and that he was upset because of the calf. He had not said a word about cruelty to Miss Sarah Louise Hathaway. I slowed down and, nibbling on a fried cake

I'd hooked from the pantry, I commenced to try to puzzle the thing out. I must have cudgeled my brains for a quarter of an hour, but I couldn't come up with it.

It occurred to me that I might ask Father about it, but something told me it would be wiser not to raise the subject. Father was not one of your begrudgers. If he had a falling out with you, he would get it set straight, and that would be that. He did not keep harking back to it once a week just to keep it warm, so to speak. I liked that in Father, and it seemed to me the best course to help him keep to his standards. So I let it rest.

But it still seemed strange that he showed more feeling for the calf than he did for Sarah Louise Hathaway.

Father was a feeling man. As editor and publisher of the Wind River *Clarion*, he was expected to have an opinion on everything from statehood, to the decline in morals, to the price of beef. He was about the most looked up to man in our town, except for Mr. Jock Moncreiff, maybe, who owned not only the bank but about half of Wyoming and everything that grazed on it.

People listened when Father spoke. Me too. And he spoke pretty plainly about how I was to put in my time now that there was no school to go to. There was no holiday in Father's thinking, and I spent long hours in the print shop out back of his office. But that was a lot better than school, according to my lights. I liked the smell of ink, and it was a game for me to lock up forms and learn to read backwards. There's lots to be learned in a school, I grant you, but a boy with his eyes and ears working can acquire a university education just musing around a print shop. With Father for a taskmaster, you'd have acquired an education whether you wanted it or not.

But Thursdays were good. That was the day the *Clarion* was published, and there wasn't a whole lot to do once I'd circulated copies around town and taken a batch to the depot. Wednesdays were tough, but Thursdays were mine from mid-morning on, which is how I came to be drifting along the main stem working over that fried cake.

As I drew abreast of the livery stable, the sound of gunfire made me jump half out of my skin. Then I grinned to myself. I knew that Sheriff Finn was pursuing his own education.

I scooted up the alley between Wong Lee's laundry and the stables and, sure enough, there was the Sheriff just re-loading his Walker Colt.

"Morning, Sheriff," I said, glad of the opportunity to watch him.

"Humph. Don't know as I should risk consortin' with known criminals," said the Sheriff, shaking his head. "Charlie Prescott, terror of schoolmarms—you are a desperate character and born to be hanged."

"Aw, Sheriff, you're funnin'."

"Not so you'd notice." He shoved a last cartridge home and spun the cylinder. "We are out one schoolmarm, and now I reckon we can look for a crime wave with all you fellers on the loose."

The Sheriff rammed his Colt into its holster. He was left-handed, and he used a peculiar cross-the-body draw, which meant that he wore his pistol on the right side, waist high and backwards, if you know what I mean. He'd set up a row of bottles on the back alley fence, and I could see he'd been busy by the amount of shattered glass littering the muddy ground.

"I kinda fancied that schoolmarm," he said, eyeing the bottles. "And if I thought that some damned biscuit-eating, egg-sucking jug-eared ribbon clerk had done me out of my chance to set up as a respectable married man—" He snaked out his pistol and near to deafened me as he blasted those bottles into a spray of multicolored shards.

"That's good shooting," I said.

He sniffed. "You should've seen me when I had my health."

"Sheriff?"

"Umf?"

"You ever kill anybody?"

"Some. They needed killin'. I take no pride in it."

"What was it like?"

"Like?" He turned and favored me with a long, calculating look. "It ain't like anything. It is about the worst feelin' on earth, I guess. You are scared and mad and all over sickish, yes, and glad, too, because it's him and not you that has gone and got dead. It is downright unpleasant, Charlie, there ain't no other word for it. No, sir. If a feller was thinkin' of goin' into the killin' trade, I would advise him to have another think."

"Well, then, what do you want to be sheriff for?"

He cleared his throat and spat, nearly drowning a horsefly that had lit on the remains of a former cat. "Somebody's got to be sheriff," he said.

"But if you don't like killing—?"

"Boy, when a man's got no education and he's got no trade, he can't be choosy. I have been a drover, an' I been a buff'lo hunter. I have trapped beaver, and once I even tried keepin' a store. It don't seem like I could ever find work that suited me."

He broke open his pistol and re-loaded. "Herdin' cows is just too lonesome, and the pay don't amount to shucks. And I hadn't no talent as a storekeeper. I went bust inside o' six weeks. Good thing, too. I was gettin' so nervious keepin' indoors all day. And then there was all that politeness.

"'Yes, Ma'am. May I recommend them onions, Ma'am. No, Ma'am, we ain't got no calico in that pattern. Could I int'rest you in a good spring tonic, Ma'am?'"

Sheriff Finn's voice took on a strangely mincing tone, and I had to snicker.

"You may laugh, Charlie," he said, biting off a chaw, "but you think about what all that counter jumpin' does to a man's spirit. I was so glad when I went bust that I gave away what was left of the stock, broke open the last keg, and I guess if I had wanted to I could have been elected mayor that very afternoon, providin' there was anyone left in that town that could stand up and vote."

He practiced drawing a few times, going into a crouch and just whipping that big left hand back and forth so fast that his arm was just a blur, as you may say. Then he straightened up and continued his chronicle.

"Now buff'lo huntin' warn't so bad. I liked the freedom of it, and not layin' in under a roof every blessit night in the year. But them green hides was so awful high that folks wouldn't stand within twenty miles o' me, leastways not downwind. So it cut into my social life considerable. And now them critters is about petered out. A man might as well try to make his livin' huntin' unicorns."

"Miss Sarah Louise Hathaway says the unicorn is a myth."

"Hmph. My opinion of Miz Sarah Louise Hathaway is sadly diminished. No unicorns?" He handed me a rusty old corned beef tin. "You toss that up and stand away."

I gave the tin a good high heave, and out jumped that Colt just barking and throwing lead. That tin took a couple or three crazy hops in the air, then dropped to the mud. I ran to fetch it.

"Four holes," I shouted.

Sheriff Finn shook his head. "Next thing you know I will be wearin' spectacles. Mebbe I should take up schoolteachin'. If I could spell, I'd try her."

He looked so disgusted that I felt sorry for him. "Why don't you wear two guns?" I said. "That way you could get off more shots at a time."

He eyed me slantways, jetted a brown stream over his shoulder and said, "It wouldn't do. I hate makin' decisions. By the time I made up my mind as to which iron to pull first, the undertaker would be jottin' down my dimensions and the choir would be tunin' up *Old Hundred*.

"No, sir, Charlie. If you was to put in for the shootin' business, the last thing you want is complications. Complications may be a good thing in the doctorin' business, and they may be a good thing in the schoolteachin' business—Say, did she really say there warn't ever no unicorns?"

"Yes, Sir."

"Damn. Boy, I don't say that Miz Sarah Louise Hathaway warn't tellin' the truth as she knew it, but I am sayin' that she plainly did not know the truth. Why, there's unicorns in the Bible. I have seen it myself. Now, are you goin' to believe the Good Book, or are you goin' to believe some little Connect-i-cut schoolmarm that talks through her nose and has got milk in her veins and is scairt of baby cows?"

"It's really in the Bible?"

"You ever know me to lie, Charlie Prescott?"

"No, Sir."

"Well, then. I say it is in the Bible. And if you will accompany me to my quarters I will just show you."

Of course I believed him. Anybody would. But I was glad of the invitation, and I trotted alongside him as he strode out of the alley.

"I reckon when you see it in Holy Writ you will realize that schoolmarms don't know as much as they let on." He pulled up short and looked down at me. "I know you ain't goin' to argue with Scripture, Charlie, but what if I was to tell you I have seen a unicorn?"

"Honest Injun?"

"And more'n that, I rode it."

My eyes must have looked like a brace of fried eggs.

"Now, I ain't ever told this to no one else, Charlie, and I would not have told you only the subject has kind of snuck up on us, and I guess I don't want to take all my secrets to the grave."

"Where'd you see him, Sheriff? What was he like? What color—"

"He was pure white, and he was the delicatest lookin' hoss I ever see. I was a drover over to Colorado about ten or a dozen years back, on a ranch owned by one o' them Britishers that has bought up about half the country.

"Well, one day out rides this citified lookin' dude that was nephew to the old feller that owned the spread. He come postin' up like them soft-bottomed lady-handed city folks does, you know, and he was astride of the purtiest, daintiest, prancin'est little pitcherbook pony in all creation.

"I never see one like it, an' I was that taken with it that I rode over bold as you please an' I says, 'What kind o' hoss might that be, Mister?'

"An' he says, 'It might be an Arabian, and it might be a unspotted pinto. But it ain't. It is a unicorn.'

"Well, Charlie, I was just that taken. But then I noticed somethin', an' I says, 'No offense, Mister, but if that hoss is a unicorn, where is his horn?'"

"He didn't have a horn?" I am sure my disappointment was in my voice.

"That's right, Charlie. That is why I ast him what I ast him."

"Well, what did he say?"

"Why, he give me a fair answer. I will say that for him for all he was a postin' up-and-down jumpin'-jack furriner. He says, 'Had to remove it, Old Boy. Got in the way of ropin'.'

"Which in course it would, don't you see, and could hurt the unicorn and spook the herd and raise all kinds of gen'ral and partic'lar hell."

I allowed that I could see that.

The Sheriff nodded. "He was pretty smart for a dude. Not everybody would have thought o' that, but would've just rode out and started a stampede and likely killed three or four drovers into the bargain."

"But you did ride him?"

"I did. That dude could see I was interested and he kindly offered me the borry of the critter for a little run."

"How'd he go, Sheriff?

"Like a prairie fire. I tell you, Charlie, that animal had more heart than a mustang. We just flew over the ground, and his gait was so smooth that even in that schoolmarmy saddle I could have rid him for a day and a half without raising a blister. Yes, Sir, if I'd had me a string of them unicorns back in St. Joe, I'd have put the Pony Express out o' business in a week."

We came to the jailhouse, and Sheriff Finn led the way in.

"Godalmighty, Blue! You skillet-lickin' son-of-a-bitch!"

I fairly hugged myself with delight as Sheriff Finn tripped over his rawboned raggy-eared hound and went into a kind of fandango to keep himself from falling on his face. Blue just got up, shook himself, and stalked over to the stove where he flopped down on his side as if he'd been shot. The sheriff hurled some pretty hard words at him, but Blue paid him no mind. He was the best and only deputy Sheriff Finn had, and no amount of language was likely to disturb him any. He went back to running rabbits in his sleep while the Sheriff went ransacking around for his Bible.

"Now where in hell did I put it?" He took up about ten pounds of notices, poster and official government papers and heaved 'em to one side. A dust storm blew up from where they landed. "I know it's around here somewhere. Just last November I—well, damnation! So that's where that pistol got to. It was here under my mendin' the whole time."

The Sheriff's "mending" was a pile of played out shirts and such that he was always going to repair but never quite got around to. The pistol he had mislaid was nothing more nor less than one of those enormous dragoon revolvers, a kind of hand-held cannon, as you may say, calculated to put a hole through an elephant, provided you could steady the thing long enough to shoot your elephant with it. That shows how much "mending" the Sheriff had accumulated, and the pile never got any smaller in my time, either.

He commenced to rattling around amongst an assortment of hardware—coffeepots, fry pans, and kettles—lifting lids and slinging things about and making such a ruckus that poor Blue finally gave it up and stalked on out of there, pausing at the door to give the

Sheriff a kind of reproachful look over his shoulder before clearing the premises.

"I hope to kiss a duck if that book ain't in this room somewheres. Stir yourself, Charlie, and see if you can't find 'er."

I had no more notion of where to look than an old maid at a kootch show tent at the county fair, but I made a show of peering under the rump-sprung armchair, the crippled bureau, and the lumpy old unmade bed against the far wall. I found considerable dust, a mortified rat that had died of old age and high living, two rimfire cartridges, a sleeve garter, some evidence of mice or other small livestock, a rusty mouth organ, but no books—unless you count a mail order catalogue from Chicago with a lot of turned down pages.

I got to my feet and commenced to banging some of the dust out of my britches, triggering a regular volley of sneezes and making my eyes water so that I could scarcely see across the room.

"Any luck?" hollered the Sheriff, who was working the shelves that held his tinned goods.

"No, Sir," I wheezed out. "Found a rat, though."

"You kill it?"

"I didn't have to."

"Oh." He pried up the lid of the flour barrel and peered in. "Dammit all, Charlie, I know I had that book right around here someplace, because when Homer Briscoe got religion and give up poker when that lantern-jawed circuit-ridin' Methodist preacher come through here last August and had that revival down to

the river bottom, he come wanderin' in here with intentions of savin' me."

"The preacher?"

"No, Briscoe, that pot-bellied, pinch-penny old
reprobate. He was goin' to save me! Here was a man
that has been cheatin' at cards and givin' short weight,
and just about starvin' his wife and children for the past
dozen years and more, and he was meanin' to save my
soul from perdition. Them was his words, mind you, not
mine.

"I says—God damn!" Sheriff Finn jammed the heel
of his hand into his mouth. "I got me a splinter! Fetch
me a needle, Charlie, off'n that table over there, in the
tin box under the coal oil jug."

I found the box all right, and under the box I found
a broken-backed Testament. "Here's your Bible, Sheriff.
I found it."

"There!" he said in triumph. "I told you it was
here, didn't I? Bring 'er here, and bring me that needle."

Sheriff Finn sat himself down and, wiping the
needle once or twice on his lapel, he squinched up his
pale blue eyes and dug in after that splinter. "Ah, that's
got the varmint. Whew! Look-a-there, Charlie. That
ain't no ornery splinter, that there is a full-growed tree."

He sucked at his wound for a bit, then took up the
tangled thread of his narrative. "So, anyway, Old
Briscoe comes in and starts to hoorawin' me about my
evil ways in gen'ral and my card playin' in partic'lar. I
let him run till he had to draw breath, and then I says,
'Briscoe, maybe you have seen the light, and maybe you
ain't. Maybe you been born again, as you say, and then

again, maybe you ain't. But if you c'n show me anywhere in the Good Book where there is a regulation agin
five-card stud, I will put on a clean shirt and come to
the mourner's bench next Sunday in front of the whole
blamed congregation.'"

"What did he say to that, Sheriff?"

"Why, what could he say, Charlie? He went into a
song and dance about gamblin' and all-round hell-
raisin', but I just turned to the Good Book here and
showed where the chosen people drawed lots to settle all
kinds of arguments. I says to him, 'Briscoe, do you allow
that the drawin' of lots is gamblin'?'

"'In a manner o' speakin',' he says, very huffy.

"'Do you allow that Aaron was a godly man?' says
I.

"'He was,' says Briscoe. 'He was high priest under
Moses.'

"'Then I got you, you psalm-singin' sanctimonious
old scutter,' says I. 'Jest take a squint at Leviticus 16:8.'
And I had 'im."

"How was that, Sheriff?"

"Read for yourself, Boy. Read it out loud."

I riffled through the Bible and found Leviticus all
right, and in 16:8 I read, "'And Aaron shall cast lots
upon the two goats, one lot for the Lord and the other
lot for the scapegoat.'"

"Read on, Charlie. You do it pretty good."

"'And Aaron shall bring the goat upon which the
Lord's lot fell . . .'"

"Ah-hah! You got that? 'The Lord's lot.' I guess
that tells you something."

"'. . . upon which the Lord's lot fell, and offer him
for a sin offering. But the goat on which the lot fell to be
the scapegoat shall be presented alive before the Lord,
to make an atonement with him, and to let him go for a
scapegoat into the wilderness.'"

"There! That did it for him, I can tell you. 'I guess
I got your goat that time, Briscoe,' I says. Next time you
come round throwin' fire and brimstone at a man, you
will make sure you know the regulations first."

"That made him back down, huh, Sheriff?"

"Not old Briscoe. He says to me, very huffy, 'That
only shows, Mr. Finn, what is generally known.'

"'Which is what?' says I.

"'That the devil can quote Scripture,' says he.

"'Briscoe,' says I, 'I am a peace officer, and a
peace-lovin' man, but I will not be spoke to in that
fashion by no sugar-sandin', dollar-shavin' counter
jumper as keeps a family on cheese parin's and mouldy
potaters and watered milk. You are a slave to Mammon,
Briscoe,' I says, 'a hard bargainer and a cheater of widders and orphans. You lay up treasure where moths cor-
rupt and thieves break in and steal. Or they would steal
only they know that me and old Blue would track 'em
down and bring 'em in.

"'No, Briscoe,' I says, 'when you give back all that
you have stole from your neighbors, including all them
card winnin's you have stole from me, and when I see
the light of Christian charity shinin' on them poor half-
starved younguns o' yours, then by gravy I will give up
all my sinful ways and put in for deacon of the Wind
River Four Square Gospel Church.'

"Well, that took the wind out of the old scutter, and he went slinkin' off like Adam leavin' the Garden. He didn't come botherin' around here for a week or more after that, I promise you."

"Did he give back his winnings?"

"Not him. Why, he was no more saved than a New York lawyer. About ten days after he'd come slithering around here tryin' to scoop up my soul, some of the boys and I was in a game over to Cassidy's, learnin' a drummer from Chicago how to play poker. Damned if old Briscoe doesn't drift in and start to hoverin' around the table like a buzzard over dead steer. He had the fever so bad he was rainin' sweat. The cards was so damp a body couldn't hardly deal 'em.

"Finally I says, 'Damn your shilly-shallyin' ways, Homer, either sit in or get out. Cast lots or cast off,' I says.

"Well, when I said that about castin' lots, that gave him his text, so to speak, and he set down and took a hand. Between us we plucked that drummer like a Christmas goose and sent him back to Chicago a sadder but wiser man.

"Old Briscoe was of a mind to pull a cork by way of celebration, but he was lookin' at me kinda wall-eyed, like he was hopin' I'd find him a text that would justify his havin' a snort. I coulda done it, too. There is a line in Second Samuel, and there is another in Timothy that would have suited his purpose, but I could see where it was leadin'. Why, it would get so that every time he was of a mind to bilk a widder or drive a debtor to ruin he would come lookin' for me to provide a text for him to hide behind. I had no time for it, and I resigned before I started.

"I says, 'Briscoe, consult your conscience, if you have one. And if you do not have one, go on instinct. Leave me out of it.'

"He got onto the bonded stuff and went rollin' home at three in the mornin' singin' *Bringing in the Sheaves* at the top of his voice and wakin' all neighbors between here and his place."

The Sheriff raised his low-crowned Stetson and scratched around in his lank sandy hair. "Briscoe left my soul alone from then on, and settled down to cheatin' and stealin' and pinchin' pennies with a light and cheerful heart.

"Why, Charlie, he hadn't no more conscience than what Blue does, and it made no more sense for him to try to reform that it would for Blue to give up fleas. It was against his nature. A man has got to be what he is, Charlie, and most of the trouble I ever see has come from folks trying to be what they ain't. It is a lot more comfortable for all hands if we can count on folks to steady down to being who and what they are."

I had the feeling that he was trying to make a point, so I tried to look wise and understanding—which, of course, was directly contrary to the point he was making. Then I said, "But what about the unicorn?"

"I was just comin' to that, Charlie. You got me off the track with all your chatter about old Briscoe. You got to learn to stick to the subject. Why, I knew a man down in Arkansas once—"

"Sheriff. The unicorn?"

"Hand me that Bible. Lemme see now. Uh-huh. Old Deuteronomy has got something to say about the critter. I knew it. Looky here, Charlie Prescott." He held the book open to me and with a broad and blackened fingernail he traced invisible lines under the text: "His horns are like the horns of unicorns."

I brightened up at that, and Sheriff Finn said, "Poor old Job has got somethin' to say about 'em, too, unless I disremember. And Isaiah. And the Book o' Numbers."

Well, by the time the Sheriff was through, Miss Sarah Louise Hathaway hadn't any standing left with either of us. And though I wished her well, and still do, wherever she might be, I hope she has taken her sign down and has given up teaching school. A lady that is that set against unicorns has got no business as an instructor of impressionable youth.

"Sheriff," I said, now thoroughly persuaded to his views on unicorns, "how come you know so much Bible?"

A wide smile creased his sunburnt face. "Surprises you, don't it, a no-account broke-down lawman knowin' his Book? Well, it was all the doin' of a good woman, a widder lady that took me in when I was a shirttail youngun not much bigger'n you. She saw to it that I warn't left in heathen darkness. She put me to readin' the Book, Charlie, an' I ain't never forgot it."

"Were you an orphan, Sheriff?"

"Good as. My mam died directly after I was born, and my pap was what you might call shiftless." The

Sheriff shook his head at the recollection. "Some folks called him a lot worse'n that."

"Did you?"

He nodded. "There was times I'd a-killed him if I'd a-dared, I reckon. But he's gone now. Been gone a long while. It ain't in me to keep a hate goin' for any considerable time. That takes more character than I got.

"I have knowed folks that has hated their whole lives. Me, I can't concentrate that long on anything. I set out to hate somebody, and next thing you know dinner's ready, or somebody says the fish are bitin', or some little commonplace thing like that, and I get distracted and fergit I am supposed to be eatin' my liver out in pure vengeance."

"But you have killed people."

"That was business." He swung his booted feet down from the chipped and battered table. "Yonder's your pa comin', Charlie. I expect he's lookin' for you."

Sure enough, the door swung in to admit Father. "There you are, Charlie," he said. "Hope he isn't bothering you any, Sheriff."

"No, Sir, Mr. Prescott. Me and Charlie has been settlin' theological questions this evenin'."

Father grinned. "I will never get used to your use of the 'evening' to describe all the hours after noon, Sheriff. It does make for some mighty long evenings."

"Comes from where I was raised, I reckon. I am too old a hoss to change now."

"Well, long or short, it is near enough to evening now to accommodate anyone's definition. Sheriff, I wonder if you'd care to drop by for supper—or dinner, if you prefer. I would like to have you meet the new school teacher."

"Aw, shoot," I said. "Already?"

I was not pleased, but the Sheriff brightened up remarkably. He said, "Well, now, Mr. Prescott, I'd be proud to break bread with you—and to meet the new schoolmarm. Just to make acquaintance, as you may say."

Father smiled. "I thought you might be interested. Mind you, it is not official yet, but given the qualifications of the candidate, I daresay the post is filled."

"Where does she stand on unicorns?" asked the Sheriff, with a wink at me.

Father looked perplexed, but decided there was a joke a-foot and let it pass. He had his own idea of humor, and was not always quick to apprehend another man's jest. Rather than be thought slow-witted, he would act as if he had not heard the joke. That way, he could not be accused of not appreciating it.

"Clara will have food on the table by 5:30, Sheriff. Charlie, perhaps you would like to stay and walk over with Sheriff Finn."

"I believe I will, Father," I said. Then I added, with what I thought was a sly look, "Is she pretty?"

Father smiled. "You will have to judge that for yourself," he said. He nodded to Sheriff Finn. "Five-thirty, then."

And he was gone.

"Stir yourself, Charlie, and find me a clean shirt," the Sheriff ordered. "I got to make myself presentable."

He bustled about, moving faster than I'd have thought was in him to do. He heated some water and stripped to his waist. He splashed and spluttered and soaped and splashed some more. Then he stropped his razor and attacked the wiry blond stubble that had been accumulating since the last Saturday night.

"You find that shirt yet?" he called, in between the dreadful rasp of his razor.

"Yes, Sir. It's on the bed."

"Well, reach into that closet and fetch down my Sunday coat."

"The one you wore to the social last year?"

"That's the one. Take the mothballs out'n the pockets and take 'er outside and wave her around to air her out some. There's a good feller."

I found the coat all right. I could have found it in the dark, it smelt so of camphor. I took it outside and did my best. But I reckoned that if I were to bury that coat in a compost heap and leave it there for three weeks, it would still come out pretty ripe.

I swung it around till my arms were ready to drop off, then came back inside where the Sheriff was standing bent-kneed before the cracked looking-glass that hung on the back wall, fussing with the part in his plastered hair.

"My goodness," I said, "what is that smell?"

"Bay Rum, mainly," he said, drawing a new line with his gap-toothed comb, "and some toilet water that I took in trade from a drummer that was passin' through here last summer."

"What did he trade you?"

"Ten days in jail."

"Oh."

"He seemed to think it was a fair trade," the Sheriff went on, turning his head first to one side, then to the other as he took a reading on that part. "That's got her, I reckon. Now lend a hand with that coat.

"Yessir," he said, as he shrugged into the shiny black alpaca garment, "that drummer was right down grateful, especially after I showed him the accommodations here. He said he judged the mattress was stuffed with corn cobs, and that the bars was sufficiently spaced to admit any amount of livestock.

"I allowed as how we was uncommonly blessed with rats lately, and that some of the prisoners had been complaining of bedbugs. I did point out that the blankets is aired regular twice in the year, and that prisoners is always complainin' anyway, it bein' their nature, but he seemed to take some stock in their grievances.

"My, this coat does set me off, if I do say it myself." He twisted himself this way and that in front of the glass, trying to get the full effect. It did look fine, for all he was so fragrant.

He took up the shirt he'd lately shucked and, placing his foot on a chair, he commenced to buffing his boots.

"Anyway," I says to that drummer, 'By rights I ought to hold you for trial, but Judge Haskell ain't due here for another ten days. That is assumin' that the stage don't break down, an' that a gullywasher don't wreck the road, an' that the judge don't fergit to show, an' that he shows up sober.

"'It might be ten days, and then again it might be a good deal longer. Why, if the stage was to be held up, or if the team was to spook and stampede, the judge might get hisself so bad hurt, if he warn't killed outright, that the Federal gov'mint would have to appoint a new judge. And by the time the President got around to interviewin' the applicants, and the Congress got around to takin' bids on the job, we might not get a new judge till 1900 or thereabouts.'"

The Sheriff buckled on his gunbelt and fetched down his 5X beaver, the one with the silver dollars set in the hatband, and set it carefully on his slicked down hair. "It was when I mentioned 1900 that the drummer remembered he had appointments in San Francisco. He suggested that it was a dreadful waste of the gov'mint's money to hold him here over a small misunderstandin'.

"'The judge, if and when a judge gets here, will only fine me,' he says. 'And the fine will hardly cover the costs of keepin' me. I am a powerful eater, Sheriff, and it takes a sight of rations to keep me in flesh. Why, if you was to hold me here ten days, I would wipe out your funds for the month.'

"He had a point. So we sat down like civilized men and we negotiated. The upshot of it was, he was to leave under cover of darkness, and I was to find that he had left behind a dozen bottles of that there toilet water. I would confiscate his goods, to be held as evidence in case he should ever turn up in these parts again."

"Evidence of what, Sheriff?"

"Why, of the crime, Charlie. He was accused of peddlin' this here toilet water as a guaranteed hair-restorer. Nate Belcher bought a bottle to try on that chestnut mare of his that had rubbed a bald place on her rump and just about ruined her looks."

"Did it grow hair?"

"Well, we can't be certain, Charlie. Nate clapped a handful on the spot, and that mare lashed out and kicked Nate right through the fence rails. She took off like her tail was a-fire and she ain't been seen since.

"When Nate recovered himself, and his liver and lights and things was all back in place, he went lookin' for that drummer. When he told him what happened, the drummer suggested that Nate might better slap a dash of the stuff on his own rump and then maybe he could run fast enough to catch up with that mare.

"That was by way of a joke, o' course, but Nate didn't think it was funny. He had his knife out and was about to carve his initials in that dude's hide when I heard the hoorawin' and busted it up and hauled that drummer off to jail.

"It is pretty strong stuff all right. Got turpentine in it, I think. It smarts pretty good when you first slap it on."

"But, Sheriff, if you use it all up, you won't have any evidence if the drummer ever comes back."

"Oh, I still got eleven bottles, Charlie. I don't hardly ever use it but for special occasions. Anyway, I reckon one bottle's as good as a dozen if I ever have to give evidence, which I doubt I will."

Sheriff Finn flicked the last speck of dust from his boots, gave a brush to his sleeves and a last tug to his shoestring tie. "We'd better mosey along, Charlie. We don't want to keep your pa waitin' supper."

"Huh. You don't want to keep the schoolmarm waiting, you mean."

"Now, looky here, Charlie Prescott, this here is what you might call an official function. It is my duty to size up newcomers and to let 'em know that we have got law here, and that we ain't backward when it comes to what is decent and regular. I am payin' this call to make myself known to the lady so she will feel secure as to person and property." He led the way out onto the street.

"Besides," he said, "I seen the way your pa smiled when you ast if she was a looker."

The Sheriff strode along so that I was obliged to half skip to keep up. Ordinarily, he moved at a sort of get-along slouch, but this night he was marching. And as he marched he gave off aromatic waves that perfumed the entire street. A snicker went up from the knot of loafers in front of Briscoe's store, but when the Sheriff halted and turned to glare, a profound silence settled over the group.

"If there is one thing I cannot abide, Charlie," he said loudly, as he looked directly at those loafers, "it is these lallygaggin' spineless spit-an'-whittle ne'er-do-wells. They got no self-respect. Why, a road agent or a bank robber or a common thief has got more character and more sand than any ten of these lowlifes.

"I tell you, Charlie, if you was to grow up to spend your time leanin' against a post and eatin' t'bacca and whittlin' sticks, you and me would have to cut acquaintance. And I guess your pa would disown you."

With a long, slow, cold look that swept the ranks of the spit-and-whittle society, Sheriff Finn shook his head and marched on. When we got to the house, the lamps were already lighted and glowing softly in the parlor windows.

I like any time of day, just so long as I am alive to enjoy it. But I am partial to lamplight time. It takes me back to quiet evenings in the old yellow house, with Father dozing behind his newspaper and Clara singing in the kitchen as she put the dinner things away. I always felt safe then, somehow, and ready to believe that somewhere the mother whose face I could scarcely remember was still watching over her boy. I still feel that way sometimes.

Well, we entered the house, and the Sheriff paused in the entry to give himself one last inspection. Then I led him into the parlor. There sat Father in his Boston rocker. Opposite him, in the green plush chair with the pineapple antimacassar, sat a man all in black. And I don't mean only his clothes, although his shirt was white enough to make a body squint. I mean the man himself was black. He was colored. He was the most dressed-up colored person I had ever seen.

"Sheriff," said my Father, looking innocent as a curly little lamb in a Sunday school picture, "Charlie, shake hands with our new schoolteacher. This is Mr. Josiah Grey."

CHAPTER II

Dinner was right down awkward. The Sheriff, his appetite unhampered by his astonishment, limited his conversation to such pearls as, "Pass them biscuits, Charlie." And I was so busy trying not to stare at Josiah Grey that all my energies were bent on controlling my eyes.

Even Clara seemed affected by the presence of our guest. She set the platters down with unwonted emphasis, raising choppy seas in the soup bowls and causing the salt cellar to skip like a young ram. When our guest presumed to compliment her on the succulence of the ham, Clara responded with a grunt worthy of a Shoshone. Father, unperturbed, presided over the roast, serving up sage observations on crops and weather with every slice and serving. It was a long meal.

"Sheriff," said my father, dropping his napkin on his plate, "I am expecting Mr. Sinclair and Major Hoxie to join us presently. Dr. Dyer will join us if his patients permit. I hope you will sit with us in the parlor while we discuss Mr. Grey's appointment."

"Proud to," said the Sheriff, forcing the words around a last mouthful of gooseberry pie.

"Charlie, you are welcome to join us," Father said, "if Mr. Grey does not object—?"

Mr. Grey smiled. "Your son and I may be working together for quite some time, Sir. It would be good for him to be present at the foundation, so to speak."

I recall how astonished I was that Mr. Grey "talked white." I don't know what I had expected, but his speech was precise and as cultured as my father's.

We'd barely seated ourselves in the parlor when Clara announced the arrival of Mr. Sinclair, the Major, and Doctor Dyer. They filed in, their combined bulk quite filling our snug best room, but the procession stopped short and their voices abruptly ceased when our callers spied the handsome black face of Josiah Grey.

"Gentlemen," said Father, leaping into the chilly void, "meet Mr. Josiah Grey, A.B., A.M., late of Harvard College in Massachusetts."

Grey rose and ever so slightly bowed. No hands were offered, none was taken.

"Is this your schoolmaster?" Mr. Sinclair's frosty eyebrows rose significantly on his corrugated brow.

"That's what we are here to determine," said Father. "Please, find seats. Coffee is on the way, and you know where the cigars are kept. Sheriff, if you will circulate the brandy—?"

When the men were fortified with drinks and smoke, Father took a stand before the Rumford stove. "As you know, we are lacking a teacher," he said, "thanks to the foolishness of certain young scoundrels whose names are well known to all of us."

Had the floor given way beneath me, I would have counted it a mercy. When I dared to raise my eyes, I found myself looking directly at Josiah Grey. His face was a perfect black blank. But before I could look away, his left eye closed in what most surely was a wink.

"Mr. Grey happened by my office this forenoon on a matter of business," Father continued, "and when I learned of his qualifications it struck me immediately that here was the very person to replace Miss Hathaway. He assures me that he is ready to open the school without delay, and I propose that we offer him the appointment."

Mr. Sinclair set his glass down and got to his feet. "Well, now, Prescott," he said, "I am a great believer in making haste slowly. Your friend has been to Harvard College, you say. And he has got some letters after his name, you say. But has he ever kept a school?"

"No, I have not," said Mr. Grey, his voice level and low.

"Hah!" said Sinclair, looking around the room for approbation of his shrewdness.

"But I was employed as a tutor in a wealthy family at New York."

"Humph. That's all very well, I am sure," said Sinclair in a tone that made plain just how far from very well he thought it was. "But keeping order in a school-house is quite another thing."

Mr. Grey yielded the point with a slight inclination of his head. "Of course," he said, "if I fail to give satisfaction, I do not expect to be kept on."

"That's fair," said Dr. Dyer, folding his large square hands over his vested paunch.

Sinclair sniffed loudly. "Are you skilled in the common branches?"

"I can take the children through higher mathematics," said Mr. Grey. "And I can teach them the use of globes, drawing, elocution, rhetoric—"

"And Latin," Father put in. "Mr. Grey is an uncommonly fine Latiner. I know you are set on sending your boy to college, Sinclair. A grounding in Caesar would be to his certain advantage."

Sinclair chewed on that for a bit. He set great store by his son, Jamie, and the prospect of a course in Latin was alluring. "I—ah, I am curious as to what brings a person of such attainments to the Territory."

"Health," said Josiah Grey.

"Perhaps you are not strong enough to manage a school," suggested the Doctor.

The black man smiled. "You are welcome to look me over, Doctor. My lungs were perhaps a bit weak, but I am sound now and only looking for decent employment to tide me over until I resume my studies."

"What studies might that be?" asked the Major.

"Medicine," replied Mr. Grey. The doctor's expression was eloquent.

Sinclair took the inquisition. "If you were to take our school, what salary do you look for?"

"The same as you would pay another."

"Generally we deduct for boarding around," Sinclair said. There was an awkward pause. "Ah—that is, we feel—felt—that because the teacher is put to no expense for food and lodging, it was fair to peg the pay accordingly."

"Perfectly fair," said Josiah Grey. "I have no objection to boarding around."

Father seemed about to strangle on a cough, and he wore a most peculiar expression.

"But that was for—maiden ladies," said Sinclair, something akin to panic in his eyes.

"Which, obviously, I am not," said Mr. Grey, smiling.

"What I mean to say is, well, boarding around might not be so convenient for you. You, ah, might want to set up late studying or—or something."

"You have a point, Mr. Sinclair," said Josiah Grey. "It might be more comfortable all around if I were to take a room at the hotel."

Major Hoxie, who owned the Empire House, looked glum. But at a look from Sinclair, he allowed that there would be tolerable accommodations at the hotel. "No smokin' in bed, mind," he grumped.

"Agreed, Sir," said Josiah Grey, sitting back in his chair and bridging his fingers just under his nose. "I use neither tobacco nor spirits, so your mind may be easy on that account."

"Are you a religious man?" asked the Doctor. "Or do you abstain for reasons of health?"

Josiah Grey looked long at the physician. Then he said, "I consider myself a Christian, Sir, if that is your meaning. I do not smoke because I do not like the taste. I do not drink because I lack the head for it."

Then he added with considerable coolness, "Are you a religious man, Doctor?"

"You are impertinent, Sir," spluttered the Doctor.

Mr. Grey nodded. "That is how your question struck me. I have put myself forward as a candidate to teach. I mean to conduct school along the lines of decency and morality as they are commonly understood. My competence to teach is open to discussion; my religious persuasion is not."

All this was said as mildly as might be imagined. There was nothing in the man's tone or in his look that could be read as hostile or abrasive. Perhaps that is why his remarks carried such force. The Doctor quizzed him no further.

"Well, then," said Father, "if you gentlemen are agreed—"

"Just a minute," said Sinclair, taking a stand in the center of the room. "See here, Grey—"

"Mister Grey."

"What?"

"I prefer to be called Mr. Grey, Sir. It is a modest prefix, but such as it is, I favor it."

Sinclair's lean cheeks went crimson. For a moment, I wished I were safely away upstairs. But he only snorted and shook his head at the "unreasonableness of some people," and carried on. "Well, Mister, then, it is all very well for us to sit here and talk about your coming to teach. And there is no denying that you are a well-spoken—person, educated and all that. But dammit, you are a—a colored man."

"That seems self-evident, Mr. Sinclair," Mr. Grey replied. "I have been aware of it longer than anyone here. What is your point? That niggers oughtn't to teach school?"

Well, there was the word, the word that had leaped in my throat when I first saw the man, the word that had no doubt crowded into the minds of the Sheriff, the Doctor, and Major Hoxie as well. Now it was out, like a bad tooth in the nip of bloody pliers. It was a relief to have it out.

Sinclair heaved a windy sigh. "You must realize that some folks might find it, well, awkward. Strange. We don't have many of your kind in these parts, and those who are here ain't able to read American, most of 'em, let alone talk Latin. It is just so out of the ordinary."

Mr. Grey nodded. "What you say is true, Sir. And had General Lee been better equipped—" He smiled and shook his head. "But that's history. And my own history is more to the point. Mr. Sinclair, you are a Scot, I take it?"

"I am."

"When did your family arrive in this country?"

"My father came over in '48 or thereabouts. Why?"

"My great-great-grandfather died fighting your countrymen. He was a freeman in the service of a militia colonel back in Connecticut. They say he killed a British officer with a whaling spear."

"A whaling spear! Good God!" cried the Major, quite pop-eyed.

"It was nothing personal, Major," said Mr. Grey. "I am sure that my ancestor would have been happy to use a musket if he had owned one."

"What is your point, man?" demanded Sinclair.

"Only that my lineage will bear scrutiny. My color must fend for itself. If I fail in my duties, you have nothing to lose. I shall be gone before you have the opportunity to discharge me."

"Come, Mr. Sinclair," said Father, "what could be fairer than that? I say we hire Mr. Grey and let him take his chances. He can do no worse than fail. And he can do no better than to fit our boys for college. We have a bargain dropped in our laps. Will you throw it away for a trifle?"

Sinclair shook his head. "It may be a trifle, and then again it may be a whole lot more. But I am game if you are, Prescott. It will be interesting to hear what Jock Moncreiff will say."

"Mr. Moncreiff has never stirred himself in the interests of this town," said Father. "Our worthy banker will have to take his chances with the rest of us."

"Very well," said Sinclair. "But don't blame me if some fool takes it into his head to burn down the schoolhouse."

"We can trust Sheriff Finn to see that that does not happen," said Father. "Right, Sheriff?"

"Huh?" The Sheriff started at being thus suddenly brought into the discussion. "Oh. Yes, Sir. I will keep an eye on the schoolhouse."

"And so will I," said Josiah Grey. "If you gentlemen have no objection, I will camp there. Then there will be no anxiety about hotels or boarding around."

"You'd save considerable money that way," said Hoxie, looking not a little relieved.

Mr. Grey smiled. "And you will be out of pocket, Major, unless someone else takes the room you had in mind for me."

The Major looked as though he had been snakebit.

"Good, then," said Father. "Mr. Grey, you may commence school on Monday. The scholars will be on hand at nine o'clock."

Mr. Grey rose. "Thank you, Mr. Prescott. Gentlemen, I will try to give full value for your money." Then he grinned. "Just out of curiosity, how much money are we talking about?"

"Well," said Major Hoxie, "we were payin' Miss Hathaway twenty dollars a month."

"But she was boarding around," put in Father.

"I was comin' to that," said the Major. "You will have the expense of your keep."

"And firewood," reminded Father. "If he is to live in the schoolhouse, we will have to double the provision for firewood."

"How does forty a month strike you?" asked the Major.

"Niggardly," said Josiah Grey.

The word was a new one to me. I thought—well, I'm not sure now what I thought. But it seems to me now that I associated it rather obviously with the man's race, and I was not altogether sure if he was saying it was nigger wages or if he was saying it was fit wages for a black man.

"You are talking about a graduate of Harvard College," Father said, "not some fugitive from honest labor who is qualified only by the muscle in his arm."

"Well, fifty, then," said Hoxie, as grudgingly as if the money were to be extracted from his own purse.

"And he can teach Latin," said Father.

"But he ain't had experience," objected Sinclair, jamming his fists into his pockets as if he would keep his own coins in place.

"Mr. Sinclair, what is the going rate for hands at your spread?" asked Father.

"Forty a month and found."

Father smiled. "And that for herding beef. We are surely able to do something handsomer for the man who will be instructing our children."

"If he can manage 'em," muttered Sinclair. "All right, Prescott, what do you propose then?"

"Sixty seems fair," said Father, "with a hundred-dollar bonus if Mr. Grey stays out the term."

"A hundred—?" Sinclair looked stricken. "A hundred dollars?"

The Doctor and the Major evidently shared Sinclair's disbelief.

"Mr. Sinclair," said Father, "if Mr. Grey can drill some Latin into our boys, he will have earned his hundred and then some. I would cheerfully write the check myself just for the pleasure—and the shock—of hearing young Charlie here read off a page of the Punic Wars.

"Besides," he added, "if you believe he will not last the term, then it becomes a sporting proposition. Why, I have known you to drop five times that sum over a turn of the cards at Cassidy's. Be a sport, Sir, and place your bet."

"Humph," grunted Sinclair. "When you put it that way, Prescott, I don't mind having a flyer. You wouldn't care to make a side wager, I suppose?"

"I am not a gambler, Sir," said Father. "But I will lay fifty dollars that Mr. Grey will last the term."

"Done," said Sinclair. He turned to Mr. Grey, a dubious look on his sharp-featured face. "You are hired, Mister. Luck to you. You will need it."

Mr. Grey bowed. "Thank you, gentlemen," he said. "This has been a most illuminating evening. I never felt so strong a bond with my forebears as when the bidding began tonight."

He offered his hand to Father. "Mr. Prescott, good night. I am beholden to you."

Father clasped the black hand. "Good night, Mr. Grey. I expect to hear great things of you."

Mr. Grey took up his hat from the sideboard, then turned to me and said, "I will count it a favor, Charles, if you will refrain from bringing any livestock into the schoolhouse. It is an unsanitary practice, and a waste of time. I am not afraid of cows."

He winked, grinned, and was gone.

"Well, Charles," said Father, "time you were in bed."

I was ready and glad to go. I went upstairs and immediately took up my listening post. The men's voices carried, and I had no difficulty in hearing them. The word "nigger" sounded a score of times in the next half hour, and it was plain that Father stood alone in his confidence in Josiah Grey.

"Folks won't take to it, Prescott," said Sinclair, in parting. "Maybe Lincoln did right, and maybe he didn't. But a piece of paper ain't going to change the way folks feel."

"Mr. Sinclair," said Father, "if I believed that, I would close down my press tomorrow and open a saloon."

Sinclair snorted like a bull at a water hole. "You'll see," he said, as Father let him out. "Latin or no Latin, no nigger is going to last a week trying to keep school here."

That opinion was passionately shared by Harney Jakes, as I discovered next morning when he and I resorted to the creek to fish for shiners.

"My paw says no old nigger is fit to keep a school," Harney said, biting off a chaw.

"He ain't old," I said. "Not real old, anyway."

"But he is a nigger."

I could not dispute that.

Harney's pale face contracted in a scowl. "Paw says if that nigger was to lay a hand on me, he will take a hosswhip to him and tear off a strip of his black hide."

"Maybe he won't lay a hand on you," I said. And I hoped that he would not. Harney may have been short on brains, but he was blocky and hard, a bullet-headed tough who maintained supremacy in the schoolyard with his fists. I don't know that he could have whipped a grown man, but he certainly was not above making the attempt.

"Well, he just better not, is all," said Harney, spitting downwind. "My paw will whip him. Or maybe my brother Rufe'll cut him some. Ain't no nigger can stand up to a Jakes, that's sure."

I felt bad for Josiah Grey.

"My paw says your paw is a nigger-lover," Harney said.

"Naw, he ain't."

"You sayin' my paw is a liar?"

I hate questions like that. In Mr. Alger's story books, the young hero is supposed to stand up to bullies, and does, and wins. But it is certain that Mr. Alger never tangled with Harney Jakes.

Harney balled up his fists and thrust forth his lower lip. "You sayin' my paw is a liar?" he said again.

"I ain't saying' anybody is a liar. I just said my father ain't a nigger-lover."

The distinction was perhaps too fine for Harney's intelligence to grasp. He was not one to split hairs, so he split my lip instead, and tripped me up and sent me sprawling. He stood over me, glowering, his drab hair in his eyes. "Git up and fight," he said.

"I am not going to fight you," I said. I am sure I presented an unheroic figure lying there, and I am sure my voice quavered shamefully.

"Scared cat," said Harney. "Scared cat nigger-lover."

I didn't argue, so Harney contented himself with a parting kick to my ribs. There wasn't much heart in it, as if it was not worth his while to waste a good kick on so worthless an object.

"There's plenty more where that come from. You tell that to your paw's pet nigger, you hear?" Harney spat in a damp display of contempt and tramped off chanting, "Scared cat nigger-lover" in a loud, unmelodious voice.

I cried a little. I am not sure why. I was not hurt, really, just ashamed. I got up and brushed off the worst of the mud and set out for home. It was yet a good two hours till dinner, so I had time to get to the house and remove the last traces of combat. And I would have made it, only I happened to run into Sheriff Finn as he was coming out of The Good Time Cafe.

"Hey, Charlie," he said, "Was you headin' for my place, by any chance?"

I hadn't been, but it seemed a comfortable idea. So I bent the facts and allowed that I was.

"I am glad of your company," said the Sheriff. "Been so blamed dull around here that I'd almost be willin' to pay somebody to rob the bank or start a fight or somethin' just to break the monotony."

He eyed me sideways and said, "You ain't heard about no fights, I suppose?"

"Oh, it was just Harney Jakes," I said. "Darned old fool."

"Busted your lip, huh?"

I nodded. A sob welled in my throat, and I didn't dare try to talk around it.

"Well, nobody never died of a split lip. You come on in and I will just dab somethin' on it. I got a salve that was give me by an old Kiowa woman that is guaranteed to cure anything from chilblains to snakebite."

He ushered me in, sat me down, splashed some water in a basin and went to work just as gentle as Clara herself could have been. Then he smeared a little bit of a sweet-smelling ointment on the cut and stood back to survey his handiwork.

"There now," he said, "I guess you will live to fight another day. Just don't put no salt on your rations tonight, and you will heal up just fine."

"Thanks, Sheriff," I said.

"My pleasure. If I had not took to lawin' I should have set up in the doctorin' line. Why, I have took out teeth and bullets, plugged up holes in fellers that was leakin' blood in a dozen places, set bones that knit up better'n new, and once I took an arm off—or what was left of it, but that don't count because the poor chap died three days after. 'Course, I hadn't no experience to speak of, and the best doctors loses patients sometimes.

"Why, one time I ketched a baby for a lady that was stranded in a mining camp in the Sierras." He shook his head at the memory of it. "It was the toughest night I ever put in, Charlie. Snow howlin' outside, only a lantern to work by, an' nothin' more'n my ignorance to go on. But that little feller turned up thrivin'. You never seen a sturdier child than what that little buster was.

"His ma wrote me a letter from clear out in Californy. I still have it around here somewheres." He surveyed the clutter surrounding us, gauged his chances of finding it, and wisely gave up. "Remind me to show it to you sometime, Charlie. It was a mighty nice letter. If I was ever to set up as a doctor, I would hang that letter on my wall, and folks would just flock in to have me tend their ailments.

"What was you an' Harney fightin' about?"

"Aw, it wasn't a fight, really. He just hit me and went away."

"For nothin'?"

"He—he said Father was a nigger-lover."

"Oh."

"Sheriff, if somebody said your father was a nigger-lover what would you do?"

"Die laughin', I guess. My pap was the most down on niggers of anybody I ever see."

"You know what I mean."

"You mean do I think you should have throwed a punch at Harney Jakes?"

I nodded.

Sheriff Finn rubbed his blond stubble with the back of his hand. "I dunno, Charlie. Seems to me there ain't nobody can tell another man when to fight and when not to. Seems like a body has to go on instinct."

"But you would never back down from a fight," I said, and my eyes began to water some.

"Wouldn't I, though?" The sheriff turned away and made a great business of sounding the depths of the enameled coffee pot. "Charlie, I would not be here today if I hadn't sense enough to back away when the deck was stacked against me. You ever hear your pa and me talkin' about that Mexican bandit they called El Lobo?"

Well, I had, of course, at least fifty times in the last five years, so I nodded, still not quite trusting my voice.

"Why, I mind the time him and his wild bunch was spotted on the road to Cimmaron. There must've been a hundred of 'em, and all packin' enough hardware to outfit a regiment. And there was me and one game-legged deputy, feller by the name of Fred Crandall.

"'Fred,' I says, when we got the news, 'now is our chance to die heroes!'

"This Crandall was a wall-eyed feller with a wart the size of a quail's egg on the end of his nose, and a pot belly, and gap betwixt his front teeth wide enough to poke a billiard cue through.

"When I said my piece, Crandall puts on his hat and coat, and he says, 'Marshal,'—I was U.S. marshal in them days—'Marshal, it is a wonderful thing for a man to die a hero, if he ain't a married man, which I am, and you are not.'

"Well, I was thunderstruck, Charlie. I had knowed Crandall for a year or more, and I never heard no talk about no wife. And I told him so.

"'Moreover, Crandall,' I says, 'I do not believe there is a female betwixt here and the Badlands that is so desperate for domesticity as to go into double harness with a man as ugly as you be.'

"It was harsh words, Charlie. I know it. But it is the truth. I have seen hosses shy when Fred Crandall come into view, and I am almost certain it was his face that spooked them steers that broke out'n the loadin' pens and tore up the main street and trampled Old Man Wyatt into a jelly and give Johnson the undertaker such a nation hard job in gatherin' up the remainders and makin' Old Man Wyatt presentable before we planted him. Johnson allus said it was his finest achievement in the undertakin' line, an' Johnson was a modest spoken man.

"Well, Crandall, he looked at me kinda sorrowful—leastways, I think he was lookin' at me. I could not be sure with that wall eye o' his—and he says, 'Drat yer dratted tin star. If I was marshal and you was deputy, you'd not talk to me in that fashion.'

"'What fashion?' says I. 'I have spoke the truth, as I was brought up to do, Crandall. You cannot fault a man for speakin' the truth.'

"'Nor do I,' says Crandall, buttoning up his coat. 'I know I am an ill-favored man, though I do not like hearing it spoke of so unvarnished like. But you have doubted my word, Marshal. You have come just shy of callin' Fred Crandall a liar. And there is widows still mournin' in Texas for men that have made that mistake before today.'

"Well, I knowed that was all bluff, of course. I have seen Fred Crandall shoot, and if he could hit a brood sow in the backside with a double-barreled shotgun at ten paces, I will kiss the sow. I was more in danger of laughin' myself to death than I was o' bein' shot by Fred Crandall. But I had spoke a bit plainly, so I made allowance and let him have his dignity.

"'Crandall,' says I, 'I do not say you are a liar. I do say that I am amazed, and more'n a mite curious. Where is this lady that has done you the honor of becomin' Missus Fred? That is what I would like to know.'"

"'She lives over in Rimrock,' says Crandall, settin' the curl in his hatbrim, 'where she keeps house for her widdered mother. If you do not believe me, Marshal, you are welcome to ride along with me and meet the lady.'

"'Well, now, Deputy,' I says, hustlin' into my coat, 'it ain't that I don't take you at your word. But I have a great curiosity to see the Belle of Rimrock Canyon.'

"So I rode out with him and, Charlie, you will not believe this, but I am here to tell you that Missus Fred was a real lady. And pretty? Oh, my. She was a little bit of a thing, no bigger'n a pistol, with copper hair and eyes as blue as them blue bonnets that them Texicans is always carryin' on about.

"There warn't much to her, but she was in charge, sure enough, and she put Fred through his paces whilst I was there—wantin' to know why he hadn't wrote, and where was the money he had promised for her ma's medicine, and was he spendin' all his time in saloons in low company.

"She kinda give me the fish-eye when she said that last bit, but I smiled real sweetly and told her how much I admired her biscuits. Wimmen is allus susceptible to flattery about their biscuits, Charlie, or so I have found.

"But this little woman wasn't havin' any. She just tossed her head like a two-year-old filly and suggested I try peddlin' that oil someplace else.

"So I told Crandall good-bye and headed over to the Indian Nation to renew acquaintance in them parts."

Sheriff Finn nodded by way of emphatic conclusion and drained off the dregs of his everlasting coffee.

"But, Sheriff," I said, "you forgot all about the Mexican bandits."

He slapped his thigh with the flat of his hand. "Them was my very words to Fred Crandall, Charlie. I was just throwin' a leg up on that strawberry roan when it struck me like a thunderclap. I stood there with one foot in the stirrup, and I says, 'Why, Deputy, I clean forgot our business back in Cimmaron.'

"'I expect it is too late to go tend to it now,' says Crandall. And I judged he was in the right of it. I had got so all-fired interested in seein' what kind o' woman would tie up with such a boogerish lookin' critter as Crandall that I'd let El Lobo and his gang go right out of my recollection.

"It was not a thing I could explain to my superiors, at least not right off. So I made up my mind to put it all in a letter first chance I got, for I made no doubt that once I put my mind to it I could do it all satisfactory.

"I climbed aboard my hoss and unpinned my badge and tossed it to Crandall. 'You can send that on to the territorial governor for me, Deputy,' I says. 'You can say a letter will follow.'

"And I rode out for the Nation."

"What did you say in the letter, Sheriff?" I said.

"What letter's that, Charlie?"

"The one you wrote to the territorial governor."

"Well, it is funny about that letter, Charlie. I was never much of a hand for writin' anyway, and by the time I got to a place where I could sit down an' give my mind to it, it all seemed kinda pointless. Five years had slipped by, the governor had retired, and El Lobo had died in a shootout with the Mexican army. I just couldn't see no advantage in spillin' all that ink over a matter which was of no interest nor of no consequence to nobody I could think of."

"So you never did stand up to El Lobo?"

"I'm here, ain't I?" Sheriff Finn winked. "If I was you, Charlie Prescott, I'd say no more about your run-in with Harney Jakes till you have had time to mull it over. Then you can put it all in a letter."

I felt better; not good, but better. Sheriff Finn had a point, but there was to my mind a considerable difference between a hundred Mexican bandits and one Harney Jakes. I couldn't quite let it go.

"But don't you think I was a coward not to fight Harney?"

"Could you beat him?"

I shook my head. "Not for another ten years. Maybe when I get my growth—"

"Then look him up when you get your growth. My land, Charlie, you have got to be level-headed. You pa is level-headed. And I judge you come from a line of level-headed people. The only reason to fight that I know of is to win. And unless you can be reasonably sure of winnin', then I say it is a fool thing to mix in it. I have knowed people to die permanently by takin' on a fight they wasn't equal to.

"I knew a boy not much bigger'n you to die in a shootin' fight—and all because his boneheaded people was too proud an' too hasty to wait for help, which they coulda had, mind you, if they'd had the sense to send for it."

The sheriff sighed. "I can still see that poor boy, Charlie, just fourteen years old, and shot plumb through in a dozen places. I have thought about him many's and many's the time over the years, and every time I do I feel just as mad and just as miserable as I done that day when I dragged his body out'n the river. I cried that day, Charlie. And it was probably my last cry, though Lord knows there's been times since when I come close.

"No, you ain't a coward, Charlie. That boy warn't a coward neither. But he's dead, and you ain't. The difference is, you got sense. And you got enough of it so you will know when it is time to take a stand, and when it is time to light out. Don't you never die tryin' to prove anything to anybody, Charlie, least of all yourself."

"When do you fight, Sheriff?"

"When there ain't no other choice." He got up and fetched his cob pipe from the rack over the stove. "If you ever got any doubts, you come talk to me. We'll sort the thing out, and if it's clear you got to fight, then by Godfreys, I will back your play. Otherwise, you keep to peaceable ways, youngun, and keep healthy. You hear me?"

"Yes, Sir."

"Good. Now run along to your dinner, and don't let me hear no more talk about cowards. There ain't none o' them in the Prescott line."

I made for the door, then turned back and said, "You reckon the schoolmaster will light out if Rufe Jakes comes for him?"

Sheriff Finn shook his head. "I dunno, Charlie. Rufe's bad medicine. There ain't no tellin' how this teacher feller might handle himself."

"He doesn't look like a fighter."

"Looks ain't in it, Charlie. They ain't no more reliable in judgin' a man than in buyin' a hoss. I have gone up against some hard cases in my time, and the worst of 'em all was a dandified little dude in Durango, a cardsharp, that obliged me to empty my pistol into him, and he still kept comin'. If I hadn't a wiped him alongside the head with my Colt, he woulda had his knife in my brisket before he died.

"And Big Red Bascombe, him that shot his way out of Wolf Canyon and killed up'ards of twenty men, he blubbered like a baby when I marched him to the gallows that July mornin' back in Ames Crossin'. He stood six foot two in his socks and dressed out at two hundred and thirty pounds, but I had to hold him up whilst they put the rope around his neck.

"I ain't a drinkin' man, Charlie, but I put away near a quart of sourmash whiskey the day they hanged Red Bascombe. It was about the awfullest thing I ever was a party to in more'n twenty years of lawin'.

"So don't go writin' off your teacher, boy. There may be more to him than a white shirt and fair speakin'. You git along home now, and make your manners to your pa for me."

I nodded, but then I had to ask one question more.

"Sheriff," I said, "what's your opinion of having a—a black man keep school?"

"Boy, you have got more questions than a railroad lawyer. You go home to your supper. We'll talk some more another day."

So I went.

Father either did not notice or did not choose to comment on my puffed lip. Dinner was our regular Saturday night fare, beans that had been simmering since before dawn, bread hot from the oven, lovely slices of perfect pork roast, and that gooseberry pie, so flaky and so juicy that no pie since has ever come close. I have spent a good part of my adult life looking for a pie like that and the woman who could bake it. It has proved a futile quest.

After dinner I had to endure the weekly ritual of a bath, alternately scalding and chilling myself in the copper tub in the kitchen. Then I reported to Clara for inspection.

"Well, I guess you got the top layer off anyhow," she conceded, after peering into my ears and surveying the back of my neck. "You c'n have a m'lasses cookie, then you say good night to your daddy and git on up them stairs to bed."

I scooped up a giant cookie and, snug in my night-shirt, perched on a stool near the gleaming stove that Clara maintained and presided over with such consummate skill.

"Clara, why don't you like Mr. Grey?" I said, watching as she rinsed the last of the plates and wiped it dry.

"Who don't like who?" She turned to me with a frown creasing her beautifully sculpted mahogany face.

"The new schoolmaster. Why don't you like him?"

Clara turned back to her work. "Who said I don't like him?"

"Oh, Clara, you know you don't. I can tell."

CHAPTER III

Sundays were a mixed blessing to me as a boy. Mornings, I'd be marched off to the Four Square Gospel Church, two big coppers clutched in my hand, a clean white handkerchief (too starched to be of any practical use) in my pocket, and my head full of instructions from Clara on how to behave within the sacred precincts.

After an hour of Sunday school instruction in the geography of Palestine and the art of ark building, I would meet Father in the churchyard and go in with him for another hour, or more, while the Reverend Owen David Owens explained what God had been doing in the intervening week, and why.

But when the service was over, and when Father and I had complied with our social duty of handshakes and Sabbath chat, there remained our ritual roundabout walk before going home to Clara and the inevitable roast chicken. Those walks are precious in my memory. I like to think that I appreciated them even then.

We would linger for a moment at Mother's grave, then strike out for the edge of town in subdued, congenial fellowship. Neighbors might nod or call a greeting, but it was understood that this time was reserved to Father and me. No one ever presumed to fall in with us on these rambles. It was a special time for me. For Father, without ever saying so, made it clear that I was free to sound him out on any theme, to ask any question, to submit any opinion, and to exercise my modest conversational powers.

I don't imagine I can do justice to Father. But I would like to make it plain that if all the fathers since Adam were lined up in a row, and I were invited to choose one for myself, I would unhesitatingly choose that same gentle soul who took those Sunday walks with me.

"Well, Charlie," said Father, as we passed the shuttered windows of Briscoe's store, "Mrs. Gaines really outdid herself on *Amazing Grace* today."

Jessica Gaines, a florid widow constructed along the lines of a young bison, invariably outdid herself, and Father unfailingly remarked on it. Mrs. Gaines had been a source of embarrassment for Father and me for some weeks after Mother's death. Her sympathy, in the form of assorted jellies and pastries, occasioned some rather general comment and speculation. It grew at last so general that Father felt obliged to suggest to Mrs. Gaines that her charity might find more fitting objects, that Clara was not likely to surrender her kitchen, that while we would always be happy to receive callers, our days were rather full and we were obliged to limit our social life rather more strictly than most folks.

Subtlety was lost on the Widow Gaines. It was not till she learned that several of her donations had found their way to the table of a tribe of impoverished Irishers that she finally got and took the hint. Her indignation was loud and public, but Father and I weathered the storm and, after the lapse of a year or so, we could pass the Widow Gaines on the street in reasonable hope of a nod in response to our greetings.

Boylike, I never wondered if Father might be lonely. He had me. And Clara kept house so well that there would be nothing for another woman to do. Long years afterward, when it at last occurred to me that Father might have married again and been happy, I did ask him about it. He smiled and said, "Only your mother could have put up with me. To any other woman I would have proved a disappointment and a bore."

And Father disliked disappointing anyone. His unfailing courtesy and his serene good nature were remarkable in a time when brawls were common, and disagreements between even men of education and position often led to blows or worse. Father sensed that it is a rare woman who can endure life yoked to a good-natured man. If he will not quarrel with her, he does not respect her—or so the feminine logic seems to run. The woman who married Father would have had to find other amusements. At the first storm signal, he'd have taken up a book or gone for a walk, and the poor woman would have taken to drink or gone mad.

Our walks regularly took us up a low rise south of town where a cluster of cottonwoods provided a shady haven on the hot afternoons of our brief summers. It was in this grove that Father had often opened his mind to me on issues that were later to be argued in his editorials. It was here that he explained to me the great mystery of male and female, and it was here that he did his gentle best to instill in me the principles that guided his own conduct and made him the most respected man in our small world.

On this particular Sunday, he quite naturally raised the subject of school. "I hope, Charlie, that you will make the most of your opportunity. Mr. Grey is a remarkable young man, and it would be a pity if you were to fool away your chance to learn from him."

"I will be good, Father," I said. "I mean to do well and to learn."

"Good boy. This is a rough country now, but you will live to see great changes and great opportunities for men of education. Statehood will come, and more people will settle here. The man who has a profession will have so much to give and to gain." He ruffled my hair with the flat of his hand. "I would not trade my time for anyone's, Charlie, but I confess that I would be more than a little interested to see what will come in your time. Just be ready for it, and see that you do not miss the parade."

"Father?"

"Yes, Charlie?"

"I don't believe that Mr. Grey will last out the term," I said, and I told him my fears of the Jakeses.

"Humph. You know that I have never tried to choose your companions for you, Charlie, but I will admit now that your associating with Harney Jakes has been a puzzle to me. We will let that pass, however—for now.

"You, ah, think that the Jakeses will drive our Mr. Grey out of the country, hey?"

"Yes, Sir."

Father nodded. "I have known three generations of Jakeses, and I am sorry to say that the breed has not improved any. Old Aaron Jakes, the grandfather, was the first person I ever knew to actually rejoice at evil.

"If you wished to make Old Aaron smile, you had only to report that another man's house had burned down, or that another man's beef had been stolen, or that another man's horse had gone lame.

"If you told him of a murder or a suicide or a fatal accident, he would hug his sides and wheeze with what I suppose you would have to call laughter. He was a thoroughly wicked old man.

"But Daddy Jakes, Reuben that is, went his father a step worse. Reuben would actually burn down the house or steal the beef himself. And it is believed that he drove his poor simple-minded wife to suicide. It is pretty certain that he has done murder more than once. Old as he is, he is not above trying it again, or I am very much mistaken."

"Why doesn't the Sheriff arrest him?" I said.

Father shook his head. "Sheriff Finn is in many ways a remarkable man, Charlie. He has had fewer opportunities and has made more of them than almost anyone I can think of. But he serves the law, and the law is a strict master. You may know a thing to be certainly so. You may have not so much as a whisper of doubt in your soul. But without evidence, without proof, the law will not let you act against the guilty. Try it, and you will find the law coming down on you with all the force of a landslide."

Father plucked up a blade of grass and nibbled on it. "When I was the age of Mr. Grey, or a bit younger, I thought seriously of reading law. But I soon realized that I could never be happy to work within such narrow boundaries.

"I have the greatest sympathy with the conscientious lawyer and lawman, Charlie, but I am glad I decided as I did. I could not bear it gracefully that such a man as Reuben Jakes could dip his hands in blood and, because of the rules of evidence, remain free."

"Well, Sheriff Finn will get him sooner or later," I said.

Father draped an arm around my shoulders and steered our steps for home. "You think highly of the Sheriff, don't you, Charlie?"

"Yes, Sir. He is the bravest and the—" I stopped short, aware perhaps for the first time in my life that comparisons can be offensive.

But Father said, "Charlie, don't ever for a moment believe that I can be hurt by your admiration for another man. Sheriff Finn is brave. He may well be the bravest man you will ever know. That has absolutely nothing to do with my love for you, or with your love for me."

"Yes, Sir," I said, feeling easier and lighter somehow.

"And I agree," Father continued as we walked on. "If anyone can catch up with Daddy Jakes, it is very likely our friend the Sheriff. Some have complained that our sheriff is careless in his manner and a bit too free in his speech. Even his friends will grant that he is not what passes these days for a gentleman. But he is something finer than that. He is a man. And I am glad that you have the good sense to admire him. He is certainly a more desirable model for you than your friend Harney."

"Harney is not my friend," I said. "He—he was just somebody to run with."

Father gave my shoulder a squeeze. "I know that there are not many boys your age here in town. But you will have to learn sometime that there are worse things than loneliness. At least I have found it to be so."

We made our way to the house in friendly silence. I got through the long afternoon quite well on my own, and I retreated to my room that night in an unusually serene state of mind for a boy who had to face the start of school come morning.

And morning came, clear and crisp and shot through with golden light. By the time I reached the schoolhouse, a fair crowd of scholars was already there. Girls were swinging on the gate or chattering under the gnarled white oak that shaded the covered well. Boys were swapping knives, playing at mumblety-peg or stoop tag, shoving, tripping, snatching caps, and capering about like so many colts let out to pasture.

My stomach contracted as I saw, and pretended not to see, Harney Jakes slouching towards me, hands in his pockets and a look of menace in his eye.

"Hey, Charlie! Charlie Prescott!"

Grateful for the distraction and the excuse, I turned to see Jamie Sinclair loping over the high-grass meadow on his pretty little white-stockinged mare.

"Hey, Jamie," I said, as the handsome tow-headed rider reined in and dismounted. "Your pa let you ride in, huh?"

"Yes," said Jamie. "The doctor says I'm fit for it. I can ride in every day now, unless we get some late snow."

"Won't make no difference, snow or no snow. This school ain't gonna keep long." Harney Jakes strutted up to unburden himself of this dire prediction.

Jamie, who at 15 was taller and broader than Harney, eyed the prophet curiously. "Why do you say that, Harney?"

Harney only nodded ominously and said, "You'll see."

Jamie shrugged. "If you say so."

"I say so." The truculence in Harney's voice was chilling to me, but Jamie seemed unimpressed. He turned to his horse and brushed the forelock out of her wide intelligent eyes.

"Ain't she a beauty, Charlie? She just flew when I gave her her head out by the salt lick. I bet she could give Major Hoxie's big bay a run for his money. I've half a mind to race him, if pa'll let me."

"Crow bait," muttered Harney, and he scuffed away.

The clang of the bell turned all eyes to the schoolhouse door where Josiah Grey, a somber figure in black broadcloth, stood waiting. Boys and girls formed separate files and straggled in, expectant and subdued.

"You may take your former places," said Mr. Grey. And when we had seated ourselves, he took up the Bible and read from Ecclesiastes:

"'To every thing there is a season, and a time to every purpose under heaven,'" he read, his voice strong and calm and low. He continued through the entire chapter, concluding, "'Wherefore I perceive that there is nothing better than that man should rejoice in his own work; for that is his portion; for who shall bring him to see what shall be after him?'"

Josiah Grey closed the book, surveyed us, his charges, and said, "The Scripture tells us that the best thing for us to do is to do our work. So let us say the Lord's Prayer, and get to work."

He led us through the prayer, then summoned us one by one up to the platform to hear us read, beginning with the smallest child and working his way through to the eldest. It was curious to me to watch him, leaning forward in his chair to catch the lisping words of the front benchers as they stumbled through their primers. His black face seemed a study in concentration and kindness, and once or twice a smile lighted his eyes as a tiny reader labored over a rough place and struggled through.

As each scholar came forward, Grey asked the child's name and he used it once or twice in correction and praise.

Young as I was, I could appreciate the contrast between the tall solid figure in black and little Mary Wentworth in her fat yellow curls and her gleaming white pinafore, her innocent neck bent earnestly over her book as with a pudgy finger she traced her way across the page.

"That was well done, Miss Mary," said Mr. Grey. "You will be a mighty reader soon, I can see. Just remember that the 'ch' in 'stomach' has the sound of 'k,' and you will do nobly tomorrow."

And little Mary Wentworth, with a smile of pure bliss, trotted happily back to her bench.

"Next scholar," called Mr. Grey. Then he interrupted himself. "Young man! You in the back row."

All eyes swiveled to the rear.

"If you will kindly put away your knife, I would appreciate it. The benches are sufficiently well decorated as they are."

Harney Jakes scowled fiercely and muttered under his breath, but he folded his Barlow knife and put it away.

Mr. Grey, either not hearing or pretending not to hear Harney's comment, called the next reader. But as that young struggler plowed along, Harney's slate somehow fell to the floor. Mr. Grey looked up, a question mirrored on his face. "What was that, please?"

"Dropped my slate," growled Harney.

"I hope it is not too heavy for you," said Mr. Grey. "Try holding it tighter, if you please."

A faint titter of laughter ran around the room, but Mr. Grey calmly turned to his visitor and continued the audition.

"'The hunter shot the beer . . .'" a small voice piped.

"'Bear,'" corrected Mr. Grey, smiling.

"My old man hunts beer," Harney remarked aloud, looking around for applause. He was rewarded with a thin, ragged volley of laughter. It stopped when Josiah Grey stood up.

"You have something to say, young man?"

"Just a joke," Harney said.

Mr. Grey nodded. "Why don't you come up here and tell it so all of us can hear?"

Harney looked puzzled. He wasn't sure Mr. Grey meant it.

"Come along," said Mr. Grey. "Do not keep us waiting."

Harney rose, deliberately knocking my books to the floor, and swaggered to the front of the room where he stood defiantly eyeing Josiah Grey.

"What is your name, please?" said Mr. Grey.

"Harney Jakes, if you want to know."

"Oh, I wanted to know. That is why I asked. Now, Harney Jakes, you will please go back and pick up the books you knocked over."

Harney looked at the teacher in disbelief. Then he looked back to where I hung half out of my seat in the very act of retrieving my books.

"And you will apologize to Charles Prescott for upsetting his things," Mr. Grey added.

Harney folded stout arms across his chest. "I don't believe I will," he said.

Mr. Grey nodded. "I rather thought you would not," he said. "A boy who displays such bad manners as you have shown us in this little while is not likely to be man enough to apologize when he has done a foolish thing."

"You callin' me a fool?" Harney's low lip stuck out, and I knew the signs. I hoped Josiah Grey did, but he seemed unconcerned—or unaware.

"No, I think it is wrong to call people fools, even when they act like fools. But I will say that you are beginning badly. I do not mean to have the good order of my school disrupted by such babyish behavior. For the last time, will you please do as I asked?"

"Not likely."

"Then you shall be punished."

"You better not use no birch on me," Harney said, taking a combative stance.

"No, Harney, the birch is for big boys. Babies must be spanked." And to the mingled surprise and delight of the scholars, Harney Jakes found himself swept up and spun around as lightly as a lady at a barn dance. Mr. Grey hauled him over his knees and thoroughly dusted his britches with a series of smartly resounding slaps. I counted a dozen; Jamie Sinclair said it was thirteen. Whatever the count, it was a memorable sight to see Harney kick and wriggle like a frightened shoat, and I confess it was a treat to hear him bawl.

When Mr. Grey let up and Harney found his feet on the floor again, he was raging. "You damned old nigger!" he cried. "You will wish you never heard of Harney Jakes before this day is over!"

And Harney bolted from the schoolhouse, trailing the tattered remnants of his dignity behind him.

I was scared now. I wanted to tell Mr. Grey to make a run for it, that he would have his hands full of Jakeses before dinner. But he called for quiet and resumed hearing us read.

I was in a sweat, and I attempted to whisper my fears to Jamie, but a warning look from Josiah Grey put a stop to that. He went calmly through our ranks and came at last to me. I went up and read straight off from my reader in a brisk workmanlike way.

"That is good, Charles," he said. "It is what I expected. You may sit."

"M-Mr. Grey?"

"Yes, Charles?"

"Well, Harney—"

Mr. Grey nodded. "I am sorry to have our first day marred by such a scene, Charles. But he needed correction."

"Yes, Sir, but—"

"I am glad you understand," said Mr. Grey. "I hope I am not a bully. I do not take pleasure in thrashing a boy. But I will do what I must to keep good order."

I wanted to warn him, but there seemed to be no way to get past that placid front. I gave it up and went back to my seat. He heard Jamie read, then Susannah

Moncreiff, 16-year-old daughter of Jock Moncreiff, who presided over the Wind River Bank and had made his pile in league with the Union Pacific Railroad.

Then Mr. Grey bid us take up our slates and he set us to work on arithmetic. We slogged along at our numbers as he circulated, checking our results. I was mortified when he reminded me that seven times eight is not sixty-five, but he did it mildly, there was no sting in it.

From arithmetic we progressed to geography, then had a rest and a crack at the water pail.

Mr. Grey consulted his silver watch. "It is now past ten o'clock. So let us have our singing lesson. I am sure you all know *Aura Lee*. I will line it out, and you all just swing right into it.

So we began, "Aura Lee, Aura Lee, maid with golden hair...."

We went through it once, and then again without lining, with Mr. Grey leading in a melodious baritone. Suddenly we were aware of a fluting soprano rising and blending with the teacher's own rich voice. It was Susannah. She was a notable singer, and was in fact the finest voice in the Four Square Gospel choir.

Josiah Grey broke into a smile and walked down from his platform to the back benches where Susannah was caroling away. Almost as if at a signal our voices trailed away, and Susannah and Mr. Grey took up a duet that was, to my unsophisticated ear, the prettiest thing I had ever heard. We sat entranced as the tall black man and the fair-haired girl gave us their song. Then we burst into a spontaneous clapping of hands.

"Miss Susannah," said Mr. Grey, "that was—"

"Nigger!" roared a voice from the schoolyard. "Git out here and take your whuppin'!"

I came very near to wetting my pants. Despite an admonition from Mr. Grey, there was a rush to the windows. I followed, but I needn't have. I knew who was there.

Mr. Grey beat a loud tattoo on his desk with his ruler. "Boys and girls, return to your places. Please."

"You better get out here, nigger," bawled the voice from the schoolyard.

Mr. Grey moved in among us and physically steered us to our benches. "Be seated, please. Sit down, Charles. Miss Susannah, please, set an example for the little ones."

His effort succeeded, at least for the moment, and when we were in our places, Mr. Grey said, "Now, I am going out to see what this is all about. Miss Susannah, I would be grateful if you would hear the little ones at their spellers. The rest of you will please keep to your work."

"Nigger!"

Mr. Grey nodded to us, then stepped to the door. "I will be back directly," he said.

As the door closed behind him, we flocked to the window. There was Harney, looking like an imp from the Pit, backed by his father and his brother Rufe. Two ornerier looking specimens than Rufe and Daddy Jakes you could not hope to find in a year of searching.

Reuben, the father, was a lank, hairy creature with what must have at one time been a hat pulled low over his eyes. His coat might have been Joseph's, it was that old, but whatever colors it may have had were long since obscured by time and weather and wear. His baggy trousers, torn at the knees, were crammed into sadly broken boots. His arms were folded across his chest, and in one grimy hand he clutched a wicked-looking braided whip that looked long enough to inspire the lead jack in a twenty-mule team.

Rufe, Harney's older brother, was dressed about as ornery as his father, only his hat had more of hat about it, and his boots, which were stolen most likely, looked nearly new. He had a pistol thrust in his waistband and an evil grin plastered over his stubbly face.

"Sweet Jesus," murmured Jamie Sinclair, peering over my shoulder, "they will murder him."

I believed it. And I was of a mind to cut and run for help, when I heard Mr. Grey speak: "You wished to see me?"

"Open the winder, Jamie," pleaded little Tom Blake. "I want to hear this."

Jamie, however, made for the door. "Let's go out and watch," he said.

"Jamie, you mustn't." Susannah Moncreiff, her face pale, her bosom heaving, spoke up from her place among the front benchers. "Mr. Grey would not like it."

Even as she spoke, Daddy Jakes bawled out, "We don't want to see you, darky. We can't bear to look at you. But we mean to teach you a lesson."

Jamie opened the door, and we all filed out onto the steps and into the yard. Mr. Grey did not turn around, but he knew we were there all right. He said,

"You children stay back. We don't want anyone to get hurt."

"Oh, yes we do," said Reuben Jakes, unfurling his whip and letting its full length trail on the sod. "We mean to hurt you, Mister High-and-Mighty Nigger Teacher, same as you done Harney."

"I tole you, you old nigger!" Harney crowed.

"Shut up, Harney," said his father, and he reached out, almost lazily, and backhanded Harney across the mouth. "We ain't here to parley; we're here to break bones."

"You can hold it right there, Reuben," cried a familiar voice. "I have got you in my sights, and I mean to drop you if you do not drop that whip."

"What are you doin' here, Finn?" cried the old man. "This don't concern you."

"I ain't here to argue, Reuben. Drop that whip, or there will be two brand-new orphans in Wind River Junction today."

With a vivid curse, Daddy Jakes flung down his whip.

"Now, Rufus," called the Sheriff, stepping out from behind the woodpile, "I will thank you to take out that pistol slow and easy and just toss it over here."

I don't know when I was ever so glad to see anybody as I was to see Sheriff Finn. He stood tall, but easy, his rifle at the ready.

"I mean now, Rufe," he said, and he levered a cartridge home.

Rufe's long fingers curled around the butt of his gun, and his eyes flashed hatred at the Sheriff.

"Nice and slow, now, Rufus," drawled the Sheriff. "I would hate to make a mistake, but I have not shot nobody since back before Christmas, and my finger is twitchin' somethin' fierce."

With elaborate slowness, Rufe Jakes unshucked his .44 and tossed it in a glinting arc so that it landed within a foot of the Sheriff's dusty boots.

"What're you buttin' in for anyway, Finn? This ain't your fight."

"I mean to see fair play, Rufe. And if you will just fork over that Arkansas toothpick you got stashed in your boot, I will back off and leave you to settle your business here. That is if you are agreeable, Schoolteacher."

Josiah Grey nodded. "Fair enough, Sheriff," he said, his voice clear and steady as if he were discussing the weather.

"Let's have it, then, Rufe. Slow, now. This here rifle is just likely to go off on her own, mind you."

Scowling horribly, Rufe bent and drew a savage looking blade from his right boot. "You got it, Finn," he said, tossing it underhand toward the woodpile.

"Fine," said the Sheriff. "Now, Reuben, if you will just take a stand over yonder by the well, we will let this discussion proceed."

As the old man retreated, Mr. Grey removed his coat and let it fall to the ground. He struck a classic fighting pose, hands high, wrists cocked, his left foot forward, his fully rounded cleanshaven chin tucked in, his eyes narrowly focused on the third button of Rufe Jakes's homespun shirt.

Rufe, his fists knotted into red-knuckled hammers, let out a wild yell and charged in.

"Bust that nigger's head, Rufe," bawled Daddy Jakes.

I heard rather than saw the blow. There came a crack like the rap of a cue ball on the break, and Rufe Jakes was down on all fours, shaking his matted locks and spraying blood over the withered grass.

"Git up, Rufus, goldarn ye. Don't you shame the fam'ly." Daddy Jakes fairly danced in his rage.

Rufe got up, none too steady on his legs, and approached his quarry with a bit more caution. Mr. Grey, his gaze riveted right where it had been, circled and circled, erect, ready, waiting. Rufe, in range, let fly with a wide swinging right. Mr. Grey's head moved back an inch or so, then his own left hand lashed out straight and true, the merest flick it seemed, and caught Rufe just under the ear. He went down again.

I cannot say for certain how many times Rufe Jakes hauled himself up out of the dust that day, but I do know that it was a mistake every time. For Mr. Grey, his white sleeves flashing in the sun, seemed to be taking target practice. He waited for Rufe to come in to him; Rufe invariable did, and a crisp short punch would bring him down.

The exhibition—it could not be called a match— took on the aspect of a show, with Mr. Grey as the graceful *artiste* and Rufe Jakes as the low buffoon. I doubt that Mr. Grey worked up a sweat; I judge that Rufe Jakes lost about a quart of blood. He was not handsome to start with; he was now raw meat. One eye was closed; he bled freely from nose and pulpy lips. A gash on his forehead let down a steady crimson stream, and I saw him spit out a tooth in a shower of bloody saliva.

We were all of us so caught up in the spectacle, just waiting to see when Rufe would finally get sense enough to stay down, that Old Daddy Jakes took us by surprise. I heard the obscene cry and the fierce whistle of the rawhide simultaneously. There was a crack like a pistol shot, and I saw Josiah Grey's hands fly to his face. He uttered a loud, inarticulate cry and slumped to the ground.

Almost reflexively, too fast for me to see it, Sheriff Finn brought Reuben Jakes down with a single shot that took the old man right through the kneecap. Rufe Jakes was floundering around on all fours, half strangled on blood and mucus. And Mr. Grey was on his knees, hunched over, blood seeping through his shielding fingers. The schoolyard looked like Missionary Ridge, and the youngest scholars were caterwauling, the girls were screeching, and the older boys were wide-eyed and dumb with fear and fascination.

I wish I could say that I ran to help Mr. Grey. I didn't. I just stood there gaping with the rest. But Susannah Moncreiff, her face deathly pale, bolted from the little porch and knelt beside the stricken teacher. She tore off her apron and tried to take his hands down so as to apply the cloth to his wound.

"No," he said, his voice muffled and hoarse, "Don't look."

"I'm not a baby," Susannah retorted. Then she turned and called to the Sheriff, who was inspecting the hole he had made in Reuben Jakes. "Never mind that trash. Come here and help me."

"Just wanted to make sure he warn't going any-where, Sis," said the Sheriff, coming over and hunkering down beside Josiah Grey. "Here, let's have a look at 'er."

The black hands came away slowly, as if reluctant to reveal the horror beneath.

"God A'mighty!" Even from where I stood I could see the color drain from the Sheriff's face. "Look away, Sis. His eye is gone. Give me that apron, and go take them younguns away. They don't want to see this."

Susannah rose, swaying like a willow. "But, Sheriff, I want to help."

"Then round up them little ones and git 'em along home. Scat, now. And tell Doc Dyer I am bringin' in some business."

Susannah backed away to where the scholars were huddled about the schoolhouse door, her eyes still on the crumpled form of Josiah Grey.

"You tads git, you hear?" cried the Sheriff, his voice angry, even fierce. "Miss Sukey, you make 'em git."

"I'll ride and warn the doctor," cried Jamie Sinclair. He dashed off and vaulted astride his little mare. He yanked her head around and drummed her sleek sides with his heels. I watched, helpless and envious, as Jamie, his hair flying, clattered out of the schoolyard.

"Charlie Prescott?" Sheriff Finn's voice brought me back to the immediate present.

"Sir?"

"My hoss is over back of the woodpile. Bring him around, quick now."

Glad of something to do, and proud that the Sheriff had called on me, I scampered off to find his tall buckskin gelding indifferently cropping the pale and lifeless grass. I led the big horse into the schoolyard and held his head while the Sheriff helped Mr. Grey to his feet.

"You just hold that cloth with your right hand, now," said Sheriff Finn, "and grasp the horn with your left. I will give you a hand up."

"I can manage it," muttered Josiah Grey, and he clambered awkwardly into the saddle.

"Stand fast," Sheriff Finn said. "I will be with you in just two shakes of a lamb's tail."

He went over to the now prone form of Rufe Jakes and got a good grip on his shirt collar. "I have seen you lookin' better, Rufe," he said, as he dragged him over to the pump. He reached down and, with a rawhide thong, he tied Rufe's wrists behind his back; then he propped him up with his back resting against the trough.

"You're next, Reuben," he called. "You want to crawl over, or do you want me to drag you?"

Reuben's reply was sulphuric. I was glad that Susannah had led the little ones away. They'd hear enough of that kind of talk before they were much older, but some of the words were new even to me, and I had thought I'd heard them all by then.

"Happy to oblige you, Reuben," declared the Sheriff, and he strode over and took that horrible old man by the scruff of the neck and the seat of the pants

and all but flung him to a place beside his barely conscious eldest son.

"God damn you to Hell, Finn!" screamed the old
man. "You have tore up my knee, and now I am goin' to
bleed to death."

"No such luck, Reuben," replied the Sheriff,
swinging Rufe around and lashing his father's wrists to
his so that the two reprobates sat back-to-back on the
sod. "I will plug up your miserable leg so that it will
hold you up on the gallows."

The Sheriff tore out the back of Rufe's shirt and
improvised a bandage for old Reuben's knee. "I put a
clean hole in you, Reuben, for which you would do well
to thank me. If I'd a-been carryin' my scattergun, you
would be a sight sicker than what you are."

He stepped back and admired his handiwork. Then
he said, "You two just sit tight, now. I got some business
in town. But I will be back directly. It pains me to leave
you, but I will be back.

"Charlie? Where did that scut Harney get to?"

I looked around; there was no sign of him. "I guess
he's run off," I said. "I wasn't noticing."

"Well, you get along home now. Tell you pa what's
happened." The Sheriff swung up behind the wounded
schoolmaster and urged his mount toward town. I
watched them go, feeling about as lonesome as a tree in
Kansas.

"You, boy."

I turned to face Reuben Jakes.

"Boy, there is a twenty-dollar gold piece in my
pocket. It's yours if you will just cut us loose and give us
a chance to git on out of the Territory."

The old man's wheedling was even more frightening than his curses had been. If the Devil made his offers in such a tone as that, we would be a nation of saints. I never heard anything so patently false, so blatantly evil.

"You seem like a nice boy. Don't he seem nice, Rufe?"

If Rufe shared his father's opinion of me, he didn't say so. He just sat, his chin sagging on his breast, his shirtfront stained with his drying blood.

"You wouldn't go off an' leave an old man, would ye, boy? Why, I could be your own grand-daddy. You couldn't leave me here to die, now could ye?"

I didn't answer. I couldn't. I just started backing away.

"Twenty dollars is a sight of money, boy. You could buy a lot o' nice things with twenty dollars."

I kept backing.

"God dammit, boy, you come here and cut us loose!" The old man stretched his corded, ropey neck like a barnyard rooster, and his wicked little eyes were bright with venom and rage. "You cut us loose, you hear?"

I turned and ran.

"I'll get you for this, you dirty little scutter!" Daddy Jakes voice rose shrill on the thin mountain air. "I'll come for ye, boy. I mean it. I will come for ye, and I mean to mark ye. I will take my knife and cut you good!"

I did not stop running till I reached my father's house.

CHAPTER IV

He has lost the sight of that eye, and he is in considerable pain," Dr. Dyer said, sitting back in the big leather-covered chair in our front parlor. "I have given him laudanum for the pain, and he is sleeping now over in my dispensary. If infection don't set it, he will be all right. Or as all right as a one-eyed man can hope to be."

Father shook his head. "I am just sick about this, George. I like that young man, and I feel responsible for him. When he wakes up, I would like to have him move in with us till he is feeling strong again."

"Might be best," allowed the Doctor.

"What makes me so angry is the senselessness of the thing. Scum like the Jakeses aren't fit to stand in the same room with Josiah Grey, and yet they mutilate him, leave him half blind, rob us of a schoolmaster—" Father raised his hands and let them fall in a gesture of helplessness.

Dr. Dyer flicked the ash from his Daniel Webster cigar. "Well, now, Prescott, don't go writing his obituary just yet. Last thing that black man said to me before he fell asleep was to tell Mr. Prescott that school would keep just as soon as he could manage it."

Father stood up, his eyes shining. "By Godfrey, Sir, it makes me proud to know him."

He turned to me and said, "Charlie, don't you ever forget this day. You have just heard what it means to be a man. It isn't guns, and it isn't fists, it is doing one's duty."

Father was really stirred up, and I reckoned I was in for a real stem-winder. He did tend to sermons, but I can think of one or two worse faults in a father. And he was sincere. I don't believe he could have been more proud of Josiah Grey if he had been blood kin.

"You see how it is, Charlie," he began—but a rap on the door halted him, and Sheriff Finn, looking about as beat as I'd ever seen him, came straggling in and plunked down on the sofa.

"If you got any o' that sourmash whisky left, Mr. Prescott, I would be nation grateful for a drop."

Father tipped the decanter and handed the Sheriff a dram. He tossed it off and wiped his mouth on the back of a gloved hand.

"Well, they got away," the Sheriff said, staring at the turkey red carpet. "I rode back out there at a hand gallop, just as soon as I'd delivered that schoolmaster to the Doctor here, and I will be damned if there was so much as a smell of a Jakes around that schoolhouse."

"But you left 'em tied up, Sheriff," I said.

"Back to back, and old Reuben with a hole in his knee, and Rufe with at least a busted snoot and a cracked jawbone." Sheriff looked angry and ashamed.

"What more could I do? I had to get that black man in. I couldn't put old Reuben on my hoss, too. And what was I to do with Rufe? Drag him in on the end of a rope?

"I wisht I had, though. Damn, but I wisht I had."

"It's beyond help now, Sheriff," said Father. "You did what you had to do. Don't go blaming yourself."

"How do you figure they pulled it off, Sheriff?" said the Doctor.

"Must a-been that Harney. Couldn't read no sign, the schoolyard was so trampled. Looked like a damn hog-waller." He fished in his britches pocket and brought out a knife. "I found this, though. It was layin' right near the pump."

"Looks like Harney's," I said. "He was cutting on his bench with it at school today."

Sheriff Finn looked glum. "Done in by a shirt-tail rat's whelp. Time I give up lawin' and took up clerkin' in a millinery store."

"Did you ride out to their shack?" Dr. Dyer said.

The Sheriff's expression was eloquent, and I would not have traded places with the Doctor just then for any amount. "I went. Even though I knowed blame well what I would find, which is what I found, which was nothin'.

"That sty was empty of Jakeses, though it wouldn't a took a bloodhound to sniff out their traces. I expect they just took out for the high country, and how far they will git is anybody's guess. Old Reuben was in no shape to travel, and Rufe warn't much better. But a Jakes is harder to kill than a diamondback rattler, and it wouldn't surprise me none if they was to turn up again when things has blown over."

"Couldn't you have tracked them, Sheriff?" The Doctor was certainly crowding his luck.

A definite reddish tinge stained the Sheriff's face and neck, and he bit off his words as he fought for control. "I could have. And they could have holed up on a ridge somewheres and picked me off whilst I was leanin' out o' the saddle to study their traces. I had hoped for a better end than bein' bushwhacked by a damned Jakes."

The Sheriff fumbled for his pipe and stuffed it with shag. "O' course," he said, scraping a match on his boot sole and applying it to his bowl, "if you was thinkin' of gettin' up a posse, Doctor, I would be proud to deputize you."

He blew out a great cloud of smoke. "'Course, I'd recommend you have your will drawed up and that you say farewell to the wife and children afore you set out. There'd be a right smart passel of widders and orphans hereabouts if we was to ride into them hills, but if you are game—"

"You have made your point, Sheriff," huffed the Doctor, hoisting himself out of his chair. "No one expects you to commit suicide."

Sheriff Finn nodded, his face uncommonly solemn. "I am proud to hear it," he said, "for it is against my principles.

"How is that schoolteacher comin' on?"

"As well as can be expected," the Doctor said, thrusting his thumbs into the armholes of his sprightly patterned vest. "With any luck, he should be up and around in a week or so."

"He is a tough citizen," murmured the Sheriff. "And fight? I tell you, gentlemen, I have seen some scrappers in my time, but I will be drowned in sheepdip if I ever see a finer boxer than what that schoolmaster is. I would back him against any man of his weight and class, bar none."

The Doctor grunted. "It is a commendable talent, I am sure. But, if you will excuse me, I had better look in on him now. I will tell him of your offer, Prescott, and if he is up to it, I will bring him over in the morning."

"Good," said Father, rising and offering his hand. "And you can tell him I would be honored to have him here."

The Doctor seemed to chew on the word 'honored' for a bit, but he got it down, nodded, and left.

"Well, Sheriff," said Father, "it is a pity those devils got away, but we are well rid of them, after all."

"For a while," said the Sheriff. "A rat will come back to his nest, Mr. Prescott. And when them villains come back, I mean to settle accounts with them. I been wantin' to make them acquainted with the warden over to the territorial prison, and it seems like introductions is long overdue."

The Sheriff stood and stretched wearily. "I am tuckered," he said. "But I will drop by tomorrow to talk with that schoolmaster."

"You need a statement from him?" Father asked.

"No, Sir. I just mean to shake his hand, and to apologize for not killing Reuben Jakes."

I just barely picked at my dinner that night. It had been a long day, and a terrible one. I kept thinking about Josiah Grey and the pain he must have been feeling. It made me feel sickish to think about his eye, and I knew that I could never forget the horror of that brutal old man and his whip.

If I slept, it was fitfully at best, and I woke with a funereal feeling in my heart. Father had gone out by the time I came down, and Clara served my hotcakes in silence. Her face was drawn and grim, and something told me it was no morning for idle conversation.

My breakfast sat in my belly like a lump of clay, and I felt no inclination to run out into the sunshine. I poked around among Father's books, but I couldn't seem to settle on any one to read.

I was slumped in Father's armchair and gnawing on a hangnail when I heard the front door swing in. Voices rose in the entry, and I heard Father say, "Come right into the parlor and we will fix you up on the sofa."

As I got to my feet, Father and Dr. Dyer, supporting Josiah Grey between them, came into the room.

"Oh, Charlie," said Father, "fetch Clara, will you? And ask her to bring sheets and things to make up a bed for Mr. Grey."

But Clara, evidently anticipating, brushed past me in the hall, her arms laden with blankets and linens. "You go 'long to the kitchen, Charlie boy, and steal some gingerbread or somethin'. Don't be underfoot."

I did not argue. One could not live long under the same roof with Clara without learning to read the signs.

And the signs that morning were unmistakable. I retreated to the kitchen and carved out a great chunk of the still warm gingerbread, poured myself a mug of milk, and sat down to gorge. But I was not to gorge alone, for no sooner had I washed down the first delicious bite when Father and the Doctor appeared in the doorway. I looked up, questioning.

"We were chased out," Father said, grinning sheepishly. "Clara cannot abide helpless menfolk in her territory."

"That isn't gingerbread, is it?" inquired Dr. Dyer, eyeing my portion with a jealous eye.

"Only the best this side of the Divide," said Father. "Take a chair, Sir, and help yourself."

The Doctor was not shy about it, I must say. His hunk was twice the size of mine, and he polished it off with amazing speed. "Good," he rumbled, spraying crumbs from under his full mustache. He dabbed around among the remains with his stubby fingers like a chicken picking up corn.

"There's more," Father said, waving the knife like a baton. And I winced to see another huge block of the gorgeous dark brown cake pass over the Doctor's horsey yellow teeth.

Luckily, Clara came stomping in just as that square went to its fate, or I might well have wept to see the Doctor come back for thirds. "He's comfortable now. You kin look in on him if you've a mind to. Only don't go unsettlin' him, and don't talk too long." Clara wiped her nose on a corner of her apron, and her eyes looked to me suspiciously bright.

"Come along, Charlie," Father said, "I am sure you will want to pay your respects."

We filed in, and now I took a real look at Josiah Grey. He lay on the sofa, his close-cropped hair in stark contrast with the snowy pillow. A white bandage covered the upper left quadrant of his face. His face was ashen, strained, scored with lines lately etched by pain. But his voice was strong as he said, "Why, hello, Charlie," and offered me his hand.

I took his hand to shake, and he held on in a firm cool grip.

"I—I am awful sorry you got hurt, Sir," I said.

He nodded. "I know you are, Charles. Thank you."

"Does it hurt a lot?"

"Charles!" Father's rebuke was spoken softly, but the edge to his voice was keen.

"It is a natural question, Mr. Prescott," Josiah Grey said. "Yes, Charlie, it hurts a lot. But I still have a perfectly good eye, thank God, and I expect to be feeling much better soon, thanks to the skill of our good physician." Mr. Grey turned his head slightly and focused his good eye on Dr. Dyer. "I am beholden to you, Sir."

Dr. Dyer was embarrassed. "It is my job," he said.

Mr. Grey smiled. "That's what I was talking about yesterday, Charlie. You see, if we do our work, we shall have our reward."

If anyone had asked me why it was at that moment that the tears came, I could not have told him. But come they did, making my eyes smart and raising a painful lump in my throat. "You had him beat fair, Sir,"

I choked out. "That damned old coward could never have hurt you without that whip."

Mr. Grey squeezed my hand. "Don't cuss, Charlie," he said. Then he grinned, a real wide open grin. "I did some cussing of my own, I will admit. You might say I have what amounts to a natural aversion to whips."

"We had better let Mr. Grey rest," said Father, "or we will have Clara down on us."

"Rest is what he needs now," Dr. Dyer said. "I will look in on you tomorrow, Grey. Er, Mr. Grey."

"Thank you." Josiah Grey released my hand and offered his own hand to the Doctor.

"Um, well, yes," sputtered the Doctor, and he clasped the black fingers for a fleeting moment, and he left.

"Charles, I am glad we shall be under the same roof for a few days," Josiah Grey said. "I hope you will come read to me sometimes."

"I will," I said. "And when you get better, could you—would you—teach me ...."

"Latin? Oh, yes, I have not forgotten."

"Well, that, too, sure. But I mean, to box."

Mr. Grey chuckled. "Charlie, Charlie, I think you are more interested in learning to hit than to conjugate. But, yes, if you father does not object—"

"Father?"

"Why, I have no objection, provided you keep up with your studies. So long as there is such a thing as a Jakes in the world, it is probably a good idea to be able to—"

"Time for Mr. Grey's medicine," announced Clara, marching in. "You two go 'long now and leave him be. He got to rest."

Father bowed whimsically. "We have our orders, Charlie," he said.

"Mr. Prescott?"

"Yes, Mr. Grey?"

"I wonder if Charles might run an errand for me?" Mr. Grey's voice rose interrogatively.

"I'd be glad to," I said. Then I added, "If you don't mind, Father."

Father nodded.

"At the schoolhouse, under my cot, there is a small wooden case with brass hinges. I would like to have it here, if I may. There are some personal items ...."

"I understand," Father said. "Charlie, you may run along now and fetch Mr. Grey's case. I must get down to the shop myself, or my new devil will be dropping frames and spilling type all over the place."

Father left by the front door and I by the back, leaving Josiah Grey to Clara's care. I felt better, better than I would have thought I could feel. Just seeing Josiah Grey and hearing him talk had dispelled my fears and chased the miseries from my brain. I loped along to the schoolhouse, sparring with the wind as I imagined how I would one day, after diligent training with Mr. Grey, square off against Harney Jakes and pound him into whimpering submission.

The schoolhouse door was not locked. It is hard to realize now, but we never locked our doors in those days. If there was a key to our house, I never saw it.

Indeed, but for the jail and the bank, I cannot recall a building in Wind River Junction that was ever bolted or barred.

It was so still and dim and cool inside. Shadows fell across the benches, but the sun, playing tag with the big-bellied clouds, threw patches of light onto the worn splintery floor. It seemed strange to be all alone in the schoolhouse, strange and just a little scary.

My footsteps were loud in my ears as I walked to the alcove where Josiah Grey had set up his modest housekeeping arrangements. In the half light I could distinguish his camp bed, the pitcher and basin on the washstand, the horsehair trunk against the wall. An eerie feeling came over me, a feeling that I was somehow intruding, and I wanted to be gone.

I knelt and groped under the cot, found the case, and rose to go. Just then I heard the squeal of hinges and a soft footfall. Someone had come in.

Ice-footed mice scampered up my spine, and I could feel my back hair rising like quills on an angry porcupine. My heart hammered in my ears as the soft steps neared. Oh, God, I thought, don't let it be Rufe. Don't let it be Harney, don't—

A shadowy figure turned the corner of the alcove and, heaven help me, I let out a yell of sheer fright. An absolute shriek rose above my cry, drowned out my shameful noise, and sliced through my taut nerves like a newly honed razor. The wooden case clattered to the floor, and I stood, limp and open-mouthed, staring at the equally terrified Susannah Moncreiff.

"Oh, sweet Jesus," she gasped, pressing her hands to her breast and leaning heavily against a corner post. "Charlie Prescott, you scared the tripe out of me."

"I don't know what makes girls so nervous," I muttered. "You ought to take a tonic or something."

"Huh! And you didn't yell, I suppose?"

"What are you doing here, anyway?" I said, prudently refusing to take up the challenge.

"I—I don't know, really. I was passing by, and I got to wondering if he—if Mr. Grey was back and maybe needed some medicine or something."

"Oh."

"And what are you doing here, Charlie? And why are you messing with his things?"

"I wasn't messing. He sent me here, if you want to know. He is staying at our house, and he wanted me to fetch this box, and—oh, Lordy, now look!" I knelt and examined the dropped case. It had broken open on impact, and some of the contents had spilled out on the floor.

"Let me help," Susannah said, kneeling beside me and pushing back a luxuriant wave of straw-colored hair.

We scrabbled around amongst the papers, letters and telegrams mostly, and bunched them together and placed them back in the box. I reached for another batch, and my fingers encountered something hard and cold.

"What have you got there, Charlie?"

"It's—it's a badge."

"Let me see."

My fingers curled around the icy metal. "No. He wouldn't want us to spy."

Susannah's hand closed over mine. "Charlie, I swear to you, no one will ever know I was here. Cross my heart. I will never breathe a word to a living soul. Let me see it, Charlie, please."

Had I been older, or more experienced with the wiles of the female, I might have resisted. If I had not been so disgustingly curious myself, who knows? I might have behaved like one of Mr. Alger's boys and covered myself with glory. But I behaved like a real boy, and I opened my hand. In the dim light we could just make out the legend on the nickel-plated shield: PINKERTON DETECTIVE AGENCY. CHICAGO.

Susannah and I stared at each other. The badge seemed to burn in my hand.

"Oh, Lordy, Charlie, what d'you suppose—?"

I shrugged in what I hoped was a manly way. "He may have found it," I said. "Maybe he is saving it. In case."

"I bet if we looked at those papers—"

"No!" For once I was sure of something. I didn't know much, but I knew we were not going to look through any papers. I gathered up everything and stowed the papers and the badge as neatly as I could in the box and clicked it shut. "It wouldn't be right, Sukey," I said.

"But aren't you curious?"

Curious? I guess. And more than that, I was confused, angry and downright disturbed. Was Mr. Grey a liar? Was he something more, or less, than what he had passed himself off as? Ten minutes before, I would have taken up his cause against all comers. Now? I just didn't know. I hated to think that he had deceived Father and me, that he was not really a Harvard scholar, a teacher, upright, noble and brave. Most of all, I hated to believe that he had been holding out on me.

"I am going home," I said. "And don't you say a word to anyone about this, Sukey. You may just start a whole lot of talk that don't amount to shucks. Mr. Grey has had trouble enough without some gossipy old girl making things worse."

"You needn't worry, Charlie," retorted Susannah, with a hoity-toity toss of her flaxen head. "I guess I know enough to keep mum."

"Well, you just better, that's all."

"Charlie, do you think I could come by and see him?" Susannah's small white hand rested on my sleeve.

"Maybe sometime. Not today. Doctor says Mr. Grey has got to rest. He ain't up to company, and he sure ain't up to questions."

"I wasn't planning to ask questions, Charlie. I just meant to be neighborly. He is my teacher, too, you know."

"I have to go," I said. "He'll be worrying about his box. You just keep mum, you hear?"

Susannah nodded and crossed her heart. "Are you going to tell him you saw it?" she asked.

"Not likely. Think I want him to know we snooped?"

"We didn't snoop. The box just fell, is all. You couldn't help it."

Well, that was true, and I felt a little kinder towards
Susannah for thinking of it.

"We'll keep his secret, Charlie," she said. "If he is a
Pinkerton—"

"Hush," I said. "He ain't. And we don't know anything about it."

Susannah nodded. "Shake on it."

We spit on our palms and struck hands.

"Charlie, you tell him I said I was sorry, all right?"

I nodded, but I didn't mean it. I wasn't planning
on saying anything. I left the schoolhouse on the run
and trotted all the way home. As I let myself in, I could
hear voices from the kitchen:

"The years creep slowly by, Lorena;
The snow is on the grass again;
The sun's low down the sky, Lorena;
The frost gleams where the flowers have been."

I tiptoed along the hall and halted at the kitchen
door. No mistake, Clara and Josiah Grey were singing.

"But the heart throbs on as warmly now
As when the summer days were nigh.
Oh! the sun can never dip so low
down affection's cloudless sky."

Their voices blended on the last plaintive note and
died away. Then I heard Mr. Grey say, "My Daddy
always said that the Yankees had the best fighters, but
the Rebs had the sweetest songs."

Clara laughed. "Lucky thing singin' don't win wars," she said.

I decided to make my presence known, so I made a noisy business of coming through the door.

"Ah, you're back, Charlie," said Mr. Grey. "You found it, I see."

I nodded and handed over the box.

"You hear us singin'?" Clara asked.

"Some," I said, "It was pretty."

"You hear that?" Clara said. "That is a boy that wants a piece of cake."

"No. No thank you, Clara. I—I don't want to spoil my dinner."

"You sick, Charlie?" Clara, hands on hips, eyed me with wonder.

"No'm, I feel fine. I—I think I will just go on up and read a while. You two just go on singing. I'll be upstairs."

I could feel Mr. Grey's eye on me as I left the room, but as I mounted the stairs I could hear their voices join again in song:

"Soft blows the breath of morning
    In my own valley fair,
  For it's there the opening roses
  With fragrance scent the air...."

I closed the door of my attic chamber, flung myself across the bed, and tried not to think of all that was boiling in my brain. I made a bad job of it, but at last, I think, I slept. I know I was startled to hear a rap on my door and a summons to dinner in my father's voice. My room was quite dark, and I was hot, confused, and a bit rattled.

"I—I will be right down," I said. I splashed water on my face, slicked down my hair, and descended the stairs, determined to make a show of cheerful normalcy. I did not manage it well.

I couldn't keep my eyes on my plate, no matter how hard I tried. And every time I looked up, Josiah Grey was looking at me. Clara bustled back and forth, humming little snatches of song, and Father seemed absorbed in the array of good things before him.

"You are off your feed this evening, Charlie," Mr. Grey remarked.

Father looked up. "Not feeling well, Charlie?"

"I am fine," I said, showing my teeth in what I hoped was a healthy smile.

"Been at the fried cakes again, I will wager," said Father, chuckling.

The very thought of a fried cake made my throat constrict.

"I—I would like to get some air," I said. "If I may be excused—"

Father looked concerned, but Mr. Grey rose and dropped his napkin onto his plate. "I was thinking the same thing," he said. "But I did not want to try my legs too severely just yet. If you would be willing to walk a little way with me, Charlie—"

I looked to Father, hoping he might veto the notion, but he only nodded and said, "Do you both good. Make room for pie."

So, feeling about as cheerful as a drunk at a temperance revival, I fetched my hat and walked out into the cool evening air, with Mr. Grey's hand weighing heavily on my shoulder. We sauntered along the wooden sidewalk, our heels thunking out a ragged, hollow beat, neither of us saying a word. I wanted to say something, anything, but I just did not know what I could say.

There was a long narrow bench in front of Briscoe's store, whittled and worn by a generation of loafers who made it their lookout, news room, and legislative chamber. It was empty now, at dinner time, and Mr. Grey steered me to it with a slight pressure of his hand.

"Let's sit, Charlie," he said. "I am none too steady on my legs, I'm afraid."

We sat for a spell, just letting the wind wash over us, not speaking, not looking at anything in particular. At least, I was very busy not looking at Josiah Grey. But I was pretty certain he was looking at me.

"I wanted to talk with you, Charlie," he said at last. "But I wanted to be particularly careful in choosing my words. Once we let a word loose, we have no way of bringing it back again. So please understand that I am trying as hard as I can to say nothing more nor less than what I mean."

"Yes, Sir," I said, feeling the misery seep into my bones.

"Fair enough." He was silent for a bit, sorting out his words, I suppose. Then he said, "Trust is just about the most important thing in a friendship, Charlie. And I will tell you straight out, I have come to think of you as my friend."

I started to speak, but he held up his hand. "Now, don't mistake me. I will still be your teacher, and I will treat you just as I would any other scholar. But I think you would expect that. I think you would want it that way."

"Yes, Sir."

"Good. Now, as a friend, I am going to have to ask you a question. I promise you, I do not want to ask it, and I would not ask it if it were not of the gravest importance. If it is unjust, if I give offense, I am sorry."

He breathed deeply, like a man about to plunge into a mountain lake, then he said, "Charlie, did you open that box I sent you to fetch today?"

"No, Sir, I didn't open it."

His arm encircled my shoulders. "Charlie, I am sorry. I—"

"But I did drop it, and it fell open. I didn't mean for it to happen, Mr. Grey. I wouldn't snoop. Really, I wouldn't."

"Sh, sh. It's all right, boy. It's all right." He patted my shoulder. "I am just glad and relieved."

"You're glad?"

"Um. It means that I can stop worrying that someone had broken into my things. And even better, I know I have a friend who will open up and tell the truth. I don't mind telling you, Charlie, when I opened that box and saw that my papers were out of order, I was about as scared as I have been since I came out to the Territory.

"It would be right down inconvenient to go about thinking that somebody had been sniffing around and going through my things. No doubt you would feel the same way if someone had been up in your room, ransacking around among your treasures. I guess you can understand how it might put a man's back up just thinking about it—and wondering, always wondering."

I allowed that I could see how that might be.

"Now, Charlie, tell me, did you by any chance look over any of the things in that box?"

I swallowed hard. Then I said, "I saw the badge."

"Pretty hard to miss it, I should think," said Mr. Grey.

There was another long silence.

"Mr. Grey?"

"Charlie?"

"You said that trust is important between friends."

"I did."

"Well, how can you be my friend if you don't trust me?"

"But I do trust you, Charlie," he protested, swinging around so as to face me straight on.

"No, Sir. No, you don't. You said you were a teacher, that you had been to Harvard College, that—"

"But that's true, Charlie. All of it. I promise you. I never lied to you, I only left out some things because I— well, in my line of work, it is just not smart to say much about anything."

"Then you are a Pinkerton?"

"Yes, Charlie. I am. And I will have to ask you to keep that interesting information under your hat. It would not be convenient to have it generally known. There are those who would not take it kindly were they to discover a detective in their midst. I do not believe they would settle for an eye, Charlie. My skin and my scalp might satisfy, but nothing less than that, certainly."

"Does Father know?

"He does. And your friend the Sheriff. And that's all, except for you and me, of course. I guess I could look the world over and not find a tighter bunch than that; not one blabbermouth amongst us. I should be able to sleep well tonight."

"How came you to be a Pinkerton?" I had to ask it.

"Well, now, Charlie, you have stirred up a long story. Let us start back to the house, and I will fill in the broad outline." He rose, a bit stiffly I thought, and we began our slow walk home.

"You have heard of Allan Pinkerton, of course."

"Yes, Sir."

"But I wonder if you have heard of Major Allan, head of the Secret Service of the Army of the Potomac."

"No, Sir."

Mr. Grey nodded. "I am not surprised. Yet he was a remarkable man, Charlie, and he had an organization of scouts who spent much of their time behind Rebel lines, collecting information for the Union side.

"My father, Corporal Homer Grey of the 54th Massachusetts, was on detached service with Major Allan's scouts in Virginia. He got himself a medal, a bullet in the shoulder, and the lady who was to become my mother—and the promise of lasting gratitude from Major Allen."

We walked on in silence for a bit, then Josiah Grey said, "My mother was a Pamunkey Indian. Her brother, my Uncle Jeff, soldiered alongside my father. It was through Uncle Jeff that my folks met."

"Then you are half-Indian," I said, fascinated by this genealogical narrative.

"About that. I can't be certain. There were a lot of Pamunkeys serving as scouts, but many of them had married with Negroes. That," he added with a chuckle, "may account for their Northern sympathies.

"However that may be, when my father was mustered out, Major Allan himself pinned that medal on him, shook him by the hand, and said that if there was ever an opportunity for him to be of service to my father, he had only to get word to Allan Pinkerton in Chicago."

"Then Major Allan—"

"Was Allan Pinkerton, yes." Mr. Grey smiled. "I used to love to hear Daddy imitate Pinkerton's way of speaking. He was a Glasgow man, from Scotland, you see, and my father could always make us laugh by mimicking the great man's speech."

"So how did you get to be a Pinkerton?"

Mr. Grey laughed. "You do stick to your points, don't you, Charlie? That's good. We will make a great scholar of you.

"Well, I was sent to school back home in Acton, and I was a good scholar. A fine Quaker gentleman took an interest in me and got me placed in an academy where I was fitted for college. He told Daddy that if I did well, he would see to it that I did not lose my opportunity. And he kept his word, Charlie. He called personally on the president of Harvard College and spoke for me. It was quite a day, I can tell you, when word got out that Homer Grey's son was bound for Harvard."

He smiled at the recollection. "Some of the young gentlemen were indignant. That was to be expected. But when President Eliot informed them that Harvard College would be able to struggle on without them if they chose to withdraw, they backed off and that was the end of it. I went, and I stayed.

"I won't deny that there were bad days, lonely days, days when I just wanted to cut and run. But I kept thinking of that bullet in my father's shoulder, and of that Quaker gentleman who was paying my fees, and I just found the grit somewhere inside me to see it through."

"And then did you join the Pinkertons?"

"No, first I went to New York as a tutor. And it was while I was there that I met Allan Pinkerton. My employer had been an officer in the Army of the Potomac, and Pinkerton was often a guest in his home when his business brought him to New York.

"I was delighted to meet him, of course, and he remembered Daddy and asked to be remembered to him, which really set me up in that household, as you can imagine."

"What was he like?"

"The Major? Keen as steel. He was not a talker, but he listened mighty hard, and his eyes were never still. He was not a big man, Charlie, not so tall as your father, but he was hard-muscled and tough as army beef. He kept his beard trimmed, and he carried himself like a soldier.

"I don't say that he was a warm man, nor a sociable man, but he was a man who commanded respect. I admired him very much.

"Perhaps he sensed that, or perhaps he just wanted to do something for my father. Whatever the reason, he and I sat up late one night while he unfolded a story of bank robbery and murder down in Mississippi. I was interested; anyone would be. But it did not occur to me that he was doing more than just talking. Then he asked me what I thought.

"Well, Charlie, would you believe it? My ideas on that case jibed exactly with his own. Before I knew what I was about, I had agreed to go on down there and have a look around. Inside of a month I was able to come up with the evidence that sent a frock-coated hypocrite to the gallows, and from that time on I have been a Pinkerton agent."

We halted before our front gate. "So you didn't really come out here for your health," I said.

Josiah Grey laughed, but his laugh was strangely hard and dry. "Oh, I am here for my health, all right. I helped to ruin a little coining scheme down in Colorado, but a couple of fish slipped through my net. If they were to find me, my health would be in jeopardy, I promise you. That is one reason why it is important that you tell no one so much as a hint of what you know."

I had to tell him. I knew it. I had known it all that evening. But I kept hoping to find a way out of it. The way never opened for me, so I said, "Mr. Grey, there is someone else who knows."

He gave a little groan. "Who'd you tell, Charlie?"

"I did not tell anyone," I said, indignant at this injustice. "She just came creeping up behind me, and it startled me so that I dropped the box, and she saw your badge."

"She? Who is she, Charlie?" Josiah Grey gripped my arms and his catlike eye bored into mine.

"That old Sukey Moncreiff," I said.

"Damn," he said, for the first and only time I ever heard him use so strong a word. "Things could not go more wrong. I think I will just have your father put my picture on the front page of his newspaper and announce to the whole country that a Pinkerton is around, and would citizens please refrain from shooting at the detective."

"I am sorry," I said. "It was not my fault. I didn't know she would be there."

Grey tried to smile. "I know that, Charlie. I don't hold you to blame. But what was she doing there? What did she say?"

"Said she was looking for you; wanted to know if you were all right. She said she wouldn't say a word about the badge or anything." And on a note of hope, I added, "She crossed her heart when she said it."

"What do you think, Charlie? Will she keep mum?"

I shrugged. "You know how girls are."

Mr. Grey snorted. "If you say so, Charlie. Still, Pinkerton himself employed female agents. And there was that actress, Pauline Cushman, that was such a help in supplying information to the Union Army. I guess she would have been dead long ago if she had not been able to keep silent."

"Old Sukey is no agent," I said. "She may be an actress, but—"

"I just wish she hadn't seen that badge." Mr. Grey sighed wearily and shook his head. He did look tired.

"Well," I said, "I don't believe she knows anybody from Colorado anyway. I am sure she doesn't know any coiners. Even if she did blab, it isn't likely to be where any of those men could hear her."

"It is not the coiners I was thinking about," said Mr. Grey. He gnawed at his upper lip for a bit, then he said, "Listen, Charlie, I have got to trust you. I know I can, and I must. I am here on a case."

"Here?"

"Yes. The railroad people have asked the Agency to look into a problem involving gold shipments."

"Oh, Father wrote about that in the paper," I said. "He said that the railroad should be more vigilant."

"Soft 'g', Charlie please."

"What?"

"The 'g' is pronounced softly, as in 'gem,' not as in 'gully.' It's 'vigilant.'"

"Oh."

"Your father has a point. And I have been trying to be vigilant myself. The trail leads here to Wind River Junction, but all I have to go on is the dying statement of one bandit who made the same mistake as Lot's wife and caught a bullet in the belly. It is pretty thin, but it is all I have. If so much as a whisper of what I am about here gets out, whoever is behind these holdups will go to ground like a hurt badger, and we will never be able to dig him out."

"I can tell Sukey to keep her mouth shut," I said.

"No, Charlie. Say nothing. Leave that to me. Your job is to continue to act as though I am only your teacher and nothing more. It will not be easy for you, knowing what you know. Secrets are horrible things to walk around with. They give a person no peace. But you will have to manage it, Charlie. I am counting on you."

We shook hands, and I vowed that I would not breathe a word, not even if put to torture or threatened with death.

"I am proud to have you on my side, Charlie," said Josiah Grey. "I know I will sleep better tonight."

Perhaps he did.

CHAPTER V

It was a relief when school commenced again. Mr. Grey, over Father's mild protest, returned to his quarters at the schoolhouse. Clara was right down angry.

"No man c'n keep house for hisself. It is against nature. You got to have hot meals and somebody to redd up the place and keep things tidy."

"If that is a proposal, Miss Clara, I am honored," said Josiah Grey, a smile playing about his mouth.

"Huh!" snorted Clara. "I guess if I was to set my cap for anybody it wouldn't be no brokendown schoolteacher with only one eye and two shirts to his name."

"I can buy another shirt."

"Never you mind," Clara said. "Jus' don't come runnin' to me when you find a button missin' or them spider bugs takes over the schoolhouse and builds webs in your coffeepot."

"Miss Clara, I know I am a fool to leave all this behind," said Mr. Grey, patting his stomach. "If I followed my own wishes in the matter, I would settle here

111

and grow old peacefully under your roof. I promise you, I have never been so well fed nor so well cared for since I left my Mama in Massachusetts back in '81."

Mollified, Clara grudgingly allowed that Mr. Grey might come by to take supper with us now and then (I had to grin when I heard her say "supper"), and that she might do some mending if she were not too beat out to tend to it.

"I call that handsome and generous," said Mr. Grey, "but I mean to pay for your trouble, Miss Clara. I am not a man to take advantage of a lady."

Clara bridled at that. "I don't take money from no two-shirt man. You can't spare it, and I don't want it."

"And I don't take charity," replied Mr. Grey, folding his powerful arms across his starched white shirt bosom.

"Looks like a Mexican stand-off," Father remarked, shooting me a wink over the rim of his coffee cup.

"We can make a barter," Clara said.

Mr. Grey nodded. "That is a good system," he said, "but what have I to trade? Surely you don't want my second shirt?"

"You c'n teach me to read an' write."

"Clara!" I said. "I didn't know—"

"Charles," said Father, "eat your pie."

"I always wished I could send a letter to my people back in Tennessee," Clara said. "And I would purely admire to be able to read the Scripture. I been a Scripture woman all my life, but I ain't ever read them blessed words for myself. It would be a glory and a comfort to me if I could just read them words right off the page."

Mr. Grey rose and went over to Clara. "Ma'am," he said, encircling her thin shoulders with his arm, "I would be proud to have you for my pupil. I will come here two evenings in the week, let us say Tuesdays and Thursdays, and you and I will sit in that wonderful kitchen of yours till we have made a scholar of you that Harvard College would be proud of."

"God bless you, Josiah Grey," muttered Clara, and she flung her apron to her face and fled.

"That," said Mr. Grey, "is a blessing I will strive to deserve."

And so Mr. Grey returned to his makeshift lodgings and to his work. I saw him daily at school, of course, and briefly at home before he would retreat to the kitchen to work with Clara. But it was not the same for me as when he had lived at our house. We were teacher and pupil at the schoolhouse and although I strove mightily to earn a word of praise from him, we virtually never spoke together alone. The business of the badge and his other self began to take on the quality of a dream. As days and weeks piled on, it became ever more difficult to associate the reserved but kindly schoolmaster with the Pinkerton agent on the track of reckless men.

It was this distance between us, I suppose, that made me susceptible to Susannah Moncreiff's abiding curiosity. She and Jamie Sinclair were my fellow Latiners, and it was our fortunate duty to remain behind each day for rigorous drill in declension and conjugation while younger scholars romped in the freedom of those brief afternoons.

"Has he said anything to you—about, you know?" That was Susannah's artful approach to her theme as we walked, more or less together, toward town, where a buckboard would be waiting for Susannah to carry her out to her father's house on the edge of town.

"We don't talk about it," I retorted, in a tone meant to imply that Josiah Grey and I were bound by a pact of manly silence.

"But he knows I know," Sukey said, her fair brows knitting in a frown. "I think I should talk to him about it. It will make him more comfortable if I tell him myself that I will keep mum."

"Don't you do it, Sukey. Just leave Mr. Grey alone. He doesn't want to be bothered by any feather-headed old girl."

Sukey looked at me with pity and scorn. "I suppose it is feather-headed to be the only one who recognized the ablative absolute today, when you wonderful, clever boys just sat there scratching your heads."

"That has nothing to do with anything," I said. It was true. Sukey was an apt scholar, and was moving through Latin grammar like Sherman through Georgia. And I did not like it much that she left Jamie and me in the dust.

"It has everything to do with it, Charlie Prescott. I am older than you, and smarter than you, and I think Mr. Grey would welcome a word from me to set his mind at ease. You've noticed how standoffish he has seemed since coming back. I heard you say so to Jamie

Sinclair just this morning. Well, it is because he is uneasy; he is fearful I will talk." Sukey fixed me with accusing eyes. "And it was you who made him fearful, more than likely."

"Oh, shoot, Sukey, I never—"

"You did. I just know it. You think you own him just because he stayed at your house for a few days. Well, he is my teacher, too, and I mean to talk to him tomorrow and let him know that I am not some ninny-hammer who cannot keep a secret.

"You do what you think best, Sukey," I said, in a show of meekness I was far from feeling. I wanted to thump her, but Father would never forgive me if I was to hit a girl. And Sukey was taller and heavier than I was.

"I do not need your permission, thank you just the same," she said, with a maddening toss of her sun-streaked mane. I wanted to kick her so bad it made my foot itch.

"I will speak to Mr. Grey about our common knowledge, and I will relieve his mind of any anxiety on that account. And," she added with what seemed to me irrelevant malice, "I will beat hell out of you and Jamie in recitation tomorrow."

"Girls shouldn't cuss," I said.

"Oh, Charlie, you are such a—a stick! I do not know why I waste my breath talking with a child."

"Well, you can just walk on by yourself, then," I retorted, "if you ain't scared that the boogerman will jump out at you."

"You," said Sukey, drawing herself up to her full height, "are a *puer stultus et parvus*. And if you don't know what that means, you may ask Mr. Grey to translate it for you."

With that, she strode off at a great rate, her massy hair bouncing at every angry step.

"Oh, *hic, haec, hoc*," I muttered, mortified that I could not think of a suitable tag to hurl after her. I watched her disappear around the bend in the path, then turned and ran back to the schoolhouse.

Josiah Grey was at his desk when I entered, feet up, just sitting and staring off at nothing at all. He swung his boots to the floor as I came in. "Oh, Charlie," he said. "What is it? Did you forget something?"

"No, Sir. I—I have something to tell you."

"Well?"

"It's Sukey Moncreiff. She means to talk to you tomorrow—about what she knows."

"Oh." Mr. Grey's voice was expressionless.

"I thought you would want to know."

He nodded, "Thank you."

"Mr. Grey?"

"Yes, Charles?"

I drew closer to the platform. "Is anything wrong?"

He smiled, and there was in his smile a weariness that bespoke heavy burdens.

"I have not been particularly cheerful, have I?"

"No, Sir. And I—well, it made me wonder if you were mad with me, or something."

Mr. Grey rose and stepped down to where I stood. "Charlie, Charlie," he said, gripping my shoulders hard, "you must not think that. I know it is unpleasant when someone falls silent and moody, but you must not look for the worst. Sometimes a man just draws into himself, or goes off on a high lonesome. That's when his friends have to be strong, strong enough to leave him alone to work out of his misery the best way he can."

"I didn't mean to trouble you," I said.

"I know. And I appreciate that. I really do. Thing is, Charlie, this business with my eye really set me back. The pain was bad enough, but now it is the feeling of always being on the prod. Every time somebody approaches me on the blind side, I just about jump out of my boots. And in my line of work it is a serious disadvantage not to have two good eyes."

I allowed that I could understand that.

"And then," he added, perching on the broad window sill and letting his legs dangle, "I get so all-fired scared of something happening to my good eye. If a piece of grit blows in under the lid, I start imagining myself back East, standing on a corner and begging for my keep.

"I couldn't stand that, Charlie. Being black is nothing to being blind. But being black and blind would just about finish me."

I like to think I was no more than ordinarily morbid for my age, but I confess that a picture of myself, sightless, flashed into my mind. I tried to imagine what it would be like, condemned to go about forever in the dark. It gave me the fantods to even consider it, so I let go of that notion and tried to think of something cheerful.

"Lots of folks get around all right on one eye," I said.

"I know, Charlie, and I expect that I will, too. It just takes a lot of getting used to, and when I am alone here in the schoolhouse I get to thinking too much. My thoughts are not the best company these days."

"Then come back to my house," I said. "Father and Clara would be glad to have you. Me too."

"I wish I could, Boy," he said, "but it wouldn't be fair to you folks. If things were to break, if word was to get out and around about me, there is just no telling what might happen. I don't believe it would be especially healthy for anyone to be found in my immediate vicinity."

The somber expression on his face slowly receded. "I should not burden you with all this, Charlie, but it does me good to talk it through. I thought I was holding up fine, but I guess the strain was starting to show.

"I kept thinking about what to tell R.P. about my eye, and wondering how I am ever to get to be a doctor, even if I live long enough to turn in my badge."

"Who is R.P.?"

"The Major's son, Robert. He runs the Agency now. I cannot think he will be pleased to hear of an agent losing half his sight in a stupid brawl."

"Does he have to know?"

Josiah Grey shrugged. Then he grinned the first real grin I had seen on his face in far too long. "You are a comfort to me, Charlie Prescott," he said. "We won't tell R.P. We will just leave him in comfortable ignorance.

And we will leave the future to fend for itself. It will be here soon enough.

"Now, what's this about Susannah?"

I related as fairly as I could what she had told me. "And when I tried to persuade her to leave you be, she called me a—a *puer stultus et parvus.*"

Josiah Grey laughed aloud. "Susannah said that, did she? The girl shows promise, I declare."

"I would like to promise her something," I muttered, stung by his laughter.

"What did you say to her?" Josiah Grey asked.

I shrugged. "I couldn't think of anything right off, at least nothing that she would not run and tell Father."

Mr. Grey roughed my hair. "Don't feel bad, Charlie. You are not the first to be trumped by a woman's tongue. Tell you what. Next time she tries an old Roman slanging match, you just tell her, '*Tellum imbelle sine ictu.*'"

"I guess I could say that," I allowed. "But what will I be saying?"

"That her words are 'a feeble dart, without force.'"

I smiled. I liked that. It had elegance. I tried it over a few times to make sure I had it right.

"I trust," said Josiah Grey, "that you can now see the value of applying yourself to your Latin."

I nodded. "It is a lot finer than telling her I hope she marries a sheepherder."

"I would say so."

"But I hope she does anyway, darned old snoop."

"Well, you leave Susannah to me. Maybe I can come out of it a little less scarred than you did, although I would not bet much on it."

"She thinks she is mighty smart, just 'cause her pa owns the bank and is such a power in the country. But she's just an old girl. You can handle her easy."

"I thank you for your confidence, Charlie. But the fact is, Susannah is mighty smart."

"She is still a girl."

Josiah Grey slid down from his perch and placed both hands on my shoulders. I looked up at him, conscious of the stark contrast of the white bandage and the black skin. "There are girls, Charlie," he said, "and there are girls. Do you think it is fair to judge all girls the same?"

"I just don't like 'em," I said.

"'*Puer stultus et parvus*,'" murmured Mr. Grey. "How do you think it must feel to be judged not for yourself but for your shell?"

I had no answer, so I did not offer one.

"What do you think of niggers, Charlie? Are they all alike?"

"Why, they all just—" And I wished I could have bit my tongue in two. I had only a moment before remarked the whiteness of the bandage in contrast with Mr. Grey's skin, and yet I had already forgot, clean forgot that he was a black man. I could feel my face flame, and I would have thanked God had the earth opened up and swallowed me.

Mr. Grey regarded my discomfiture without emotion. "People call me a nigger, Charlie. People make up their minds about me before I say so much as 'Good morning.' They take one look, and they already know exactly what to expect."

"But you're different."

"Everybody is different, Charlie. Everybody." He sighed. "Lord, Boy, if I could teach you that, it would be more important to you—and to all the people you are going to meet—than Latin or Greek or all the facts in all the books in all the libraries of the world."

I felt solemn and sheepish and cheap. And I guess it showed. Mr. Grey cupped my chin in his cool hand and raised my face to meet his gaze. "You have a feeling heart, Charlie. That's good. You are young, and you are ignorant, but time will take care of that. Just you try to remember what I told you. It is God's own truth, Charlie, and it may spare you a lot of grief one day if you will just hold on to it."

"I will," I said.

Mr. Grey nodded. "Good. Now, then, I do believe you had better be getting along home to your supper."

"Aren't you coming, too?"

"Good Lord!" Mr. Grey struck his forehead with the heel of his hand. "It is Tuesday, isn't it? Miss Clara will be expecting me. Let me just collect the tools of my trade, and we will walk along together."

Josiah Grey scooped up a few books and a slate and crammed them into a baize bag. He seemed to hesitate for a moment, then retreated to his alcove. He reappeared shortly, strapping a gunbelt around his trim waist. I am certain my eyes widened some at the sight of the hardware, for he smiled and said, "I may be growing overly cautious in my old age, Charlie, but Mr. Colt's peacemaker may prove a comfort to me on the long walk home."

He shrugged on a loose-fitting duster and we set forth in the deepening twilight.

"Won't that coat hamper your draw?" I asked, as we rambled toward town.

"I am not a fast-draw artist, Charlie. I subscribe to Mr. Wyatt Earp's theory; the battle belongs to the man who takes his time. If I am obliged to use this thing—which I earnestly hope I shall not be—I mean to get as near as I can to my adversary before I thumb my hammer back.

"Cartridges are dear, and Mr. Robert Pinkerton has a true Scot's abhorrence of waste. Besides," he added, with something like his old grin, "I doubt I could hit anything smaller than a full grown steer outside a range of thirty paces."

"Sheriff Finn says he dropped a bandit at forty yards once, down in Texas."

"With a pistol?"

"Yes, Sir. Remington Army .44."

"It is possible. It is a good weapon, and the Sheriff is a mighty shooter. But even he would allow that luck was with him that day, I think. Meaning no disrespect to the Sheriff.

"But if I knew I was walking into trouble, I would feel a lot more cheerful carrying my old Henry .44 rifle. And a cut-down .10 gauge scattergun would give me the confidence of a Faro dealer with a marked deck."

"Shucks, that's no kind of shooting," I said.

"Well, it is loud, and it is untidy, but it will get the job done. I remember one of our agents, a Captain Lull, who packed a handsome English-made .43 caliber pistol. He went up against John Younger with it, and he was found just as dead as if he had been carrying that pea-shooter I relieved you of last week. It may not be stylish, Charlie, but a shotgun is persuasive."

"It just doesn't seem sporting—"

"Sporting!" Josiah Grey snorted like a draft horse. "Sporting is when you shoot pigeons on the wing. We are talking about a bird that can shoot back—or shoot first, if he has got the edge. No, sir, Charlie, there is no sport in it. I hope that you are never in such circumstances, but if ever you are obliged to throw down on a man, just remember your wife and children, and do what has to be done."

"I don't mean to have a wife," I said.

"Then remember your insurance company," he said, laughing.

I could see he was just not of a mind to talk sensibly, so I gave it up. But I was certain that Sheriff Finn would not stoop to using a shotgun, not if he was to face the Daltons, the James gang and the Youngers simultaneously. It seemed to me then that Mr. Grey would do well to stick to keeping school.

Dinner that night was actually merry. Father got off a few new jokes he'd borrowed from a fancy-goods drummer from St. Louis. I thought them pretty poor, but Mr. Grey laughed so hard that the cups jumped in their saucers.

When the table was clear, he and Clara withdrew into the kitchen, and I could hear only a vague murmuring as Clara labored through her assigned pages in the McGuffey's reader. For my own part, I seated myself at the dining room table and pored over my Latin book, hoping to find more ammunition to fire at Sukey Moncreiff.

Towards nine o'clock, Mr. Grey emerged from the kitchen, a piece of cake in his hand and an arm around Clara's unyielding waist. Father, drowsing in the lamplit parlor, looked up with a smile.

"Mr. Prescott," said Josiah Grey, "take a good look at this lady. She has gone through the first, second, third *and* fourth reader in no more than three weeks. Is that a champion? I leave it to you."

Father rose and let his paper slip to the floor. "Clara," he said, lowering his spectacles from his high, smooth forehead, "I am just that proud of you."

Clara was embarrassed, but proud, too. "It ain't—"

"Isn't."

She nodded to Mr. Grey. "—isn't hard once someone points out the ways of letters, how they can be soft one time and hard the next, and how one letter can have different sounds. Once you learn that, it is as easy as making gravy."

"Well, you have a fine teacher," Father said.

Clara nodded. "He'll do. For a two-shirt man."

Mr. Grey pretended to be put out. "Well, now, Miss Clara, I was all set to start you on Latin. But you can just go find yourself a three-shirt man. I have my pride, too, you know."

"Latin? Glory be!" said Clara, laughing. "I got enough trouble just learning American. No, thank you, Mr. Grey. I will content myself—"

But here there came a sharp rapping at our front door.

At Father's nod, I went to the door and admitted Sheriff Finn. He charged straight into the parlor without so much as a "Howdy."

"They got it," he said, disgust ringing in his voice. "They just ignored our decoy, let it roll right by and never showed a hair. But when the second train come, they went for it like buzzards to a dead steer."

"They got the shipment, then," Father said.

"They did. Killed a guard, near to brained the fireman, and scooped up any amount of gewgaws and loose cash from the passengers. I tell you, Mr. Prescott, it just beats all how them scutters does it."

"Same pattern?"

"Yes, sir. There was rocks piled on the tracks and the telegraph operator swingin' his lantern—"

"With a pistol clapped to his head, I take it," said Josiah Grey.

"So he says." The Sheriff rubbed his chin with the back of a gloved hand. "What makes me so damn' mad is, they knew. They knew that first run was a trap. We had ten men sittin' in the express car, all of 'em armed with enough hardware to start our own regiment, and they never got so much as a smell of them robbers. There's a leak somewheres, Mr. Prescott. There ain't no other way on God's earth to account for it."

"What do you think, Mr. Grey?" asked Father.

Grey nodded. "The Sheriff is in the right of it. The run to Cheyenne last month was known about all over the Territory. But tonight's run was so hastily arranged that there wasn't time to get word around. And the decoy train was known only to the committee."

"Huh," grunted the Sheriff. "That don't say a whole lot. Most of them men has got wives or their fancy ladies over to—"

"Charles," said Father, noticing me at last, "it is time you were upstairs."

A protest rose to my lips, but with the Sheriff and Mr. Grey there, I could not risk my standing. Besides, I knew I would not miss much, provided I hurried. So I said my good-nights and went off peaceably, then scampered to my listening post to continue my education.

"As I was sayin'," resumed the Sheriff, "it wasn't a bad notion to try to limit the circle. I can't fault the notion."

"Thank you." Josiah Grey's voice was arid.

"But is contrary to human nature for people to keep things to themselves. You got to figure that for every person that is in on a secret, you add two more. And them two, being only mortals, can be relied on to leak to two more a-piece. So, by the time you get around to shippin' your gold or your silver or your—"

"Your point is well taken, Sheriff," said Father, breaking in. "People will talk."

"That's it exactly, Mr. Prescott. I knowed you would see it, being older and more experienced. Now, you take a feller that is new to the ways of folks and is only just startin' out in his trade. He might calc'late that people will be wise enough to keep mum so as to give us a show at findin' out who the informer is. Why, if everyone was to keep mum—which they would not, bein' human, you see—it would be easy as tic-tac-toe three-in-a-row. We would know for certain that someone from the committee is in cahoots with them desperadoes, and we could narrow our search accordingly."

"You do not seem to have much faith in your committee," Father began.

"My committee?" The Sheriff snorted. "It is no committee of mine, Mr. Prescott. I do not hold with committees. I hold with shrewd watching and bold action. And I play a lone hand."

"While you were playing your lone hand," said Mr. Grey, "there have been four robberies in as many months, and three men killed, and some eighty thousand dollars taken."

"What are you suggesting, Mr. Pinkerton Man?"

"I am suggesting that you are mule-headed, opinionated, old-fashioned—"

"Old-fashioned!" roared the Sheriff.

"Gentlemen," said Father.

"Old-fashioned and set in your ways," continued Mr. Grey, as coolly as if he were calling the roll at the schoolhouse, "and purely determined not to be shown up by an upstart nigger in a collar and a tie."

"Gentlemen," said Father again.

"Just a minute, Mr. Prescott," said Sheriff Finn, his voice crackling with anger. "Let's get this thing out on the table."

"Fine," said Father. "But let us do it calmly. There is no need to wake the house—or the town, for that matter. Speak your piece, Sheriff, but softly. Please."

There was a long silence and I pressed my ear hard against the grating for fear of missing so much as a syllable. Then the Sheriff said, "I will admit I do not take it kindly when some Johnny-come-lately takes it on himself to pass judgment on the way I do my job. I was chasin' renegades through the Texas brush when some people had not yet cut their first tooth. And I have nailed my share of hides to barn doors from here to Helena.

"As to these here train robberies, I admit I can't point to no progress. But there has been Wells Fargo men and railroad detectives and Federal officers and Pinkertons in on it, too, and I don't know that they have come up with anything that looks like a clue nor a culprit neither."

"I will grant you that," said Mr. Grey.

"Now, there is one more thing I have got to get said. Then I will button up and let someone else do the talking.

"I will tell you straight out, Mr. Detective, that I do not take pleasure in explanations and excuses, but you have raised the business of color which, I will remind you, I never did."

"Granted again," said Mr. Grey.

"That fact is, I am Missouri born and bred. I have known your people all my life, and there was some that was mean, and some that was low, and some that hadn't no more sense than God give geese.

"But it is also a fact that I have a great kindness towards your people that goes back to a time before you was even thought about."

"Your old Mammy, I suppose," said Mr. Grey.

"God damn your know-it-all highfalutin' Harvard College ways!" I heard the Sheriff's hand smack the table hard. "I never had no mammy, nor no ma neither, as far as I can remember. I was born poor and raised poor, and I expect I will die poor. I didn't own no slaves before the war, and I don't hold with them that runs around troubling black folks now. I will go down the road with any man, black or red or brown or yeller, just so long as he holds up his end, and so long as he don't get in the way when the shootin' starts."

I heard the sound of a chair being shoved back.

"I will say good night now, Mr. Prescott," said the Sheriff. "When you and this—Pinkerton has decided what is your pleasure in the matter of roundin' up them robbers, you can just slip a note under my door and tell me when to have the cells ready. I will lock 'em up any time you fetch 'em in."

"Sheriff," said my father.

"Sir?"

"Have the goodness to sit down and stop acting like a jackass."

"Hear, hear!" cried Mr. Grey.

"And you, Sir," said Father, "will oblige me by acting like the gentleman I took you for."

It got very quiet, and I was glad to be up where I was. When Father took that tone, what you wanted to do was to climb the nearest tree, and then ask what was the matter. I pitied the Sheriff and Mr. Grey.

"I am moved to say it," Father went on. "I am disappointed in you—both of you. I had thought, Sheriff, that you were too old a horse to let some youngster get your back up. And you, Mr. Grey, you were surely brought up to better ways. Sheriff Finn is an old and honored friend, and as fairminded a man as you are likely to meet in the Territory."

"I am sorry," said Mr. Grey.

But Father bored in, just as he always did with me. I loved my father, but I will say that he was a hard man to stop once he got up a head of steam. "You don't know it, Mr. Grey, and Sheriff Finn would never tell you, but the fact is, he actually risked his own freedom by helping a runaway slave get to the Free States back before Fort Sumter."

I wished I could see Mr. Grey's face, but I imagine my own was something to behold. I was always learning something new and remarkable about our Sheriff, seemed like. I certainly would never have taken him for an abolitionist.

That same thought popped into Mr. Grey's brain, and he spoke it about the same way I had framed it in my own head.

"I never was no abolitionist," allowed the Sheriff, his tone a bit grudging but less belligerent. "I never was nothing. I never joined no church, nor no party, nor no lodge. I never run across one of them outfits that was so hard up for members that they would take me. Besides, I was only an ignorant shoeless child, and I didn't give a dead rat for the politics of it, nor the morals, nor the consequences."

"Then what on earth did you do it for?" asked Josiah Grey.

"For friendship," said the Sheriff. "Now, if you don't mind—"

"I believe I had the floor, Sheriff," Father said. "And I will not give it up until you two pigheaded mules give over, shake hands, and get on with the business that brought us here."

"I will be proud to shake your hand, Sheriff," said Josiah Grey. "And I ask your pardon."

"Well, you can't say fairer 'n that, I guess," allowed the Sheriff. "I guess I rode you a little rough there myself. I didn't mean no harm by it."

Father released a windy sigh. "Now, then, the night is sliding along, and we have got to address ourselves to what is, and never mind what ought to be. The fact is, there is a Judas on the committee, or there is a loose-lipped fool. Either way, we must smoke him out and shut him up."

"Agreed," said Josiah Grey. "But how?"

"As the Injun said to the mermaid," muttered the Sheriff.

I heard laughter, but I was a couple of years figuring out what it was they were laughing at. It didn't matter. I was glad to hear them laughing. I never could and still can't abide it when friends—or folks who ought to be friends—get all huffy and standoffish. We are here for such a little while, it makes no sense for us to be any more hurt or lonely than we absolutely have to be.

"Hem!" said Father, recovering both his dignity and the floor. "It is probably our best line to try some discreet questioning. If we were to sound out the men individually and in private, we might develop a lead that would take us somewhere."

"I do not see how I can help there," said Josiah Grey. "As far as they know, I am just the schoolmaster. And I do not think any of them would be likely to open up with me in any case."

"You are right, Mr. Grey. But I think we would do well to keep your present identity intact. You just keep your ears open as you go about the town. You just might pick up something useful."

"I c'n tackle Sinclair," volunteered the Sheriff. "I got to ride out to his place t'morra anyway. There's a new rider showed up at his place, and I mean to have a look at him."

"Good enough," said Father. "I am going to interview Jock Moncreiff tomorrow, for a statement for the *Clarion*. And I can always find an excuse to look in on Dr. Dyer."

"I'd look in on the Doctor's wife if I was you," said the Sheriff. "She is a woman that could talk the secrets out of a corpse. In fact, the corpse would invent secrets to tell her just so's he could have some peace."

Father laughed. "Cora is an awesome woman, I will admit. If the Doctor has said anything to her, it is already on its way to the Eastern papers."

"*Cherchez la femme*, eh?" said Josiah Grey.

"Come again," said the Sheriff.

"It's French for 'look for the woman,'" Father said. "It is a way of saying that whenever there is trouble, you will find a woman at the bottom of it."

"Didn't know them Frenchmen had so much sense," said the Sheriff. "I knowed a squaw man once, a French feller. He was the foolishest—"

"I think I had better look in on Briscoe, too," Father went on. "He is ordinarily closer than a fat man's vest, but he has got a wife."

"So did that French feller I was telling you of," said the Sheriff. "A Paiute woman, she was, uglier than an Army mule and big around as a full-growed grizzly."

"Moncreiff hasn't got a wife, anyway," said Father, "and only the one child."

"Funny you should mention children," went on the Sheriff. "That Paiute lady produced a child every blessit year, just as reg'lar as breathin'."

"Remarkable," said Mr. Grey.

"And that was includin' the year when that Frenchy was away the whole twelve months, up in the high country. When he come back and found there was another new face at the table, he was troubled in his mind."

"What did the lady have to say for herself?" asked Mr. Grey, plainly interested now.

"Why, she said it was the way of the Injun wimmen. That a white lady might carry a child only the three quarters, but that Injun wimmen sometimes take as much as a year to bring one along."

"Did he believe her?" asked Mr. Grey.

"He had his doubts. Matter o' fact, he asked me about it, knowin' that I was a man knowledgeable in Injun ways."

Father was caught. "What did you tell him, Sheriff?" he said.

"Why, I said that Injun ways are not white ways, and that I was personally acquainted with a Oglala Sioux who was 14 months in the making, and he dressed out at near to three hundred pound and stood near seven feet high on account of bein' so long in the oven."

"And he believed you?"

"Don't you?"

Father laughed. "I believe that it is a wise father that knows his own child."

"I think you have the sayin' back'ards," said the Sheriff.

"But appropriate to the case," said Josiah Grey. "I believe that I could pick that Frenchman's child out of a crowd."

"Tow-headed?" suggested Father.

"And perhaps a sprinkling of freckles across the nose," said Mr. Grey.

"A nose with a decided tilt, I will wager," said Father.

"By Godfrey Moses," said the Sheriff. "You have described the pup as well as if you seen his tintype."

"Uncanny," said Father.

"Remarkable," said Mr. Grey.

"Have I told you this story before?" demanded the Sheriff.

"I expect you must have," Father said.

"A sure sign of old age," said Josiah Grey. "Once a man takes to repeating himself, it is only a few short steps to the front porch and the rocking chair."

"Have your fun," growled the Sheriff. "We will see who is ready for the rocking chair when once we get a lead on them bandits."

"Well, we are not gaining on them by sitting up all night. Sheriff, you and I have our work cut out for us. And Mr. Grey, if you are to face those eager scholars of yours come morning, I suggest that we adjourn in favor of a night's sleep."

There was a general scraping of chairs and a rumbling of goodnights. I scooted to bed and snuggled down under the blankets, shivering myself warm. I heard Father's heavy tread upon the stair, the rattle of his door latch, the protesting creak of his bedstead, and the muted clump of his boots hitting the floor. Then, oddly, I heard his door open again, and his voice came floating up the attic ladder: "Good night, Charles. You can go to sleep now."

When I re-entered my skin, I called down a good night and burrowed into my pillow.

From far below, down along the darkling street, someone was whistling an old song. The melancholy music faded as the walker sauntered to the edge of town, but not before I recognized the strains of *Aura Lee*.

CHAPTER VI

> "As a blackbird in the spring,
> 'Neath the willow tree
> Sat and piped I heard him sing
> In praise of Aura Lee ....."

Sweet and clear the song rose on the early morning air as I trudged up the lane leading to the schoolhouse. I recognized her voice, of course. I'd have known it anywhere. But what, I wondered, was Sukey Moncreiff doing at the school so early? And I was annoyed, for I had wanted a private crack at Mr. Grey myself, which was why I had made it a point to be up and out a full half hour before my usual time.

The door was open, and I could hear now the husking sound of the corn broom whisking over the wide-board floor.

> "Aura Lee, Aura Lee,
> Maid with golden hair,
> Sunshine came along with thee,
> And swallows in the air."

"Golden hair! Plain old yellow, she means," I muttered to myself. My sour reflections were not sweetened when I heard another familiar voice take up the verse:

"Take this heart and take this ring
I give my all to thee.
Take me for eternity,
Dearest Aura Lee."

Both voices then swung into the chorus, and I swung back up the lane and nearly broke my toe when I lashed out with a savage kick at the bole of a budding cottonwood.

What did Sukey think she was doing? And what on earth was Josiah Grey thinking of? This was no time for singing lessons. Besides, I had serious matters to discuss, and I couldn't very well discuss anything in front of hateful Sukey Moncreiff and her blasted golden hair.

I was mad, I admit it. I thought seriously of just hooking school altogether and wandering off to console myself with the promise of that spring morning. But Wednesdays were half-days anyway, and according to my logic, I would be hanged just as high for hooking a half-day as for hooking a whole one. So it seemed like poor odds to risk wrath at home, and perhaps a hiding at school, for a mere fifty percent crime.

I tramped down to the brook and squatted on a cold stone to sulk. Somehow, I sulked longer than I'd meant to, and I was startled to hear the clanging of the bell that summoned the scholars in. I got up a little too quickly, went all over dizzy, and slid into the brook up over my boots. Lord, that water was cold!

Thoroughly mad now, and feeling about as foolish as I'd ever felt in all my life before, I clambered out and went sloshing up the bank towards the schoolyard. And of course I slipped, and of course I fell, and made an unholy rent in the knee of my britches. Right then, for ten cents cash or scrip, I'd have sold out and gone to California. I tell you, I was boiling.

I charged head down across the schoolyard, thundered up the steps, and went banging through the door like a young steer coming out of the chute at the fairgrounds. A score of heads swung around at once, and from the look on those faces, I must have appeared quite a desperate character as I hove into view.

"Charlie?" Mr. Grey's tone was mildly questioning.

"Well?" If my feet were cold, my head was not, and that 'well' burst out with a violence that astonished even me.

"You are tardy," said Mr. Grey.

"I fell in the darned old brook," I said.

A giggle broke out in the ranks, but Mr. Grey rapped for silence. "The brook is where you had no business to be," he said. "You may sit by the stove till you are dry.

"I ain't that wet," I said. "I will just take my reg'lar—"

Charles!"

"Sir?"

"Sit by the stove."

I glared at him with hate in my heart, but he only stared back out of his one good eye, and I knew that I could not defy him except at a price which I was not prepared to pay. My feet squished in my boots as I stumped to the stove, and my face flamed as the sniggering broke out once more. I wanted to hit someone, and I wasn't particular as to age, size or gender. But there was no opportunity, not there, not then. I slumped into the visitor's chair near the cast-iron stove, and gave myself over to thoughts of vengeance.

It was a long morning. Mr. Grey called on me to recite, and I lied and muttered, "Not prepared."

"Please remain after dismissal, Charlie," said Mr. Grey, just as calmly as if he were asking me to fill the water pail.

I have had better days.

The hours to dismissal dragged along. Others recited or sang or worked sums. I sat, cloaked in mortification and seething in the hot broth of injustice, staring sullenly at the floor and wishing with all my heart that I had drowned in the brook.

The wish magnified into a fancy, and the fancy into a vivid drama of imagination. I saw my pale waterlogged self being retrieved from the chill waters, saw the solemn procession to the churchyard, saw my grieving mates—inconsolable now as they suffered the horrors of remorse for having ever laughed at me, saw Mr. Grey at the mercy of his guilty conscience, saw the Reverend Owen David Owens scatter the funereal dust on the lid of my small coffin, saw Clara sobbing into her apron, saw Father—

A great sob welled up in my throat and a burning tear spilled over onto my cheek. It was so unspeakably sad. And it would serve them right. Too late, they would come to visit my grave; too late would the repentant Sukey lay flowers on the raw mound above my bones.

So lost was I in this deliciously morbid spectacle that the dismissal bell jarred me like a slap to the ear. There was a general shuffling and scuffling as the exodus began. I felt the gentle pressure of Jamie Sinclair's hand on my arm as he passed by, but I did not look up. Susannah lingered at Mr. Grey's desk for some minutes, then she swung on up the aisle, her book clutched to her breast.

"Good night, Charlie," she said, as she passed by, and it was all I could do to refrain from tripping her. How I wished that for just five minutes the law against punching girls would be repealed. But I had to content myself with renewing my abiding hope that she would end by marrying a sheepherder and live out her life in disgraced exile somewhere in the remotest wilds of Montana.

It was quiet now, uncomfortably so. But I was resolute. I would not look up. I would not be the first to speak. I could hear the sound of the departing scholars fading in the distance, and the assorted rustles and clicks of Mr. Grey's tidying up. I continued to focus my gaze on the floor. Then I heard the measured tread of approaching feet. My eyes slid sideways and lit on the square, polished toes of the teacher's boots.

"Well, now, Charlie," said Mr. Grey. "Would you care to tell me what is troubling you?"

I did not trust myself to speak. I was not so certain now myself just what it was that had set me off. It had all seemed so clear to me at the time, but now all I could manage was a shrug.

"Oh," said Mr. Grey. "It's like that, is it?"

I felt seven times a fool.

"You know, Charlie, when friends have a misunderstanding, it is not fair and it is certainly not helpful to go all huffy and cold. Seems to me that friends have a duty to set each other straight when an offense is given—or taken. Otherwise, that friendship is going to just shrivel up and die.

"Now, I would have thought that you were the kind of friend who could look his friend straight in the eye and let him know exactly what it is that has put a burr under your saddle.

"Was I wrong, Charlie? Was I?"

I raised my gaze to meet his, and in his patient face I read an expression of genuine concern. My eyes began to water, and I felt myself perilously near to blubbering. But I wouldn't. I'd exhausted my quota of foolishness for one day, and I did not mean to run up a debit.

"I—well, I can't make any sense out of it myself, now," I said, swallowing hard and forcing myself to keep my voice low. "Maybe I need a tonic."

Mr. Grey threw back his head and laughed. "Charlie, Charlie," he said, dropping down onto a scholar's bench, "so it is sulphur-and-molasses time."

I grinned sheepishly. "Must be," I said.

"And is that why you went scampering off to the brook instead of coming in when you arrived so early?"

"You saw me?"

He tapped the black patch that now covered his sightless eye. "Don't let this fool you, Charlie," he said. "A one-eyed cat can still catch mice. And this good eye of mine does double duty these days. I saw you scooting up the rise, and I had a notion then that something was sticking in your craw."

I had recourse to another shrug.

"Of course, it could be that you are just having a bad day. Happens to everybody. We wake up mad and we just stay mad all day long. No one can talk to us, and nothing can please us. All we can do is hunker down and weather the storm. I know what that's like.

"Did you wake up mad this morning?"

"No, Sir."

"Hm. Then the cause must lie elsewhere. Let me try my Pinkerton skills. You woke up in a reasonable frame of mind. You set off for the schoolhouse. Anything happen along the way to set you off? A fight? An argument?"

I shook my head.

"Then it has to be—" He snapped his fingers with a sound like a pistol shot. "Susannah!"

Mr. Grey cocked his head and eyed me quizzically.

"Charlie, you haven't gone and got yourself stuck on Susannah, have you?"

My face must have given my feelings away, for he burst out laughing and said, "You look as though you have swallowed a hoptoad, live and kicking. Is it so far-fetched as all that? Lots of boys have found themselves taken with the charms of an older female. And Susannah is not without charm."

"Some people seem to think so," I muttered. I wanted to point out that it was not I who was caroling away about golden hair and all that slush, but I didn't care to crowd my luck.

"I think so, Charlie," said Mr. Grey, rising and looking steadily down at me. "She is a bright, charming girl and a fine scholar. And she knows that I am a Pinkerton."

The sun broke through. Of course! That was it. Mr. Grey had to put up with her. He could not risk making her angry by chasing her away. She'd talk for spite, and in no time the whole country would know his secret. Any chance he'd have of nailing the robbers would go right down the spout.

I lightened up something wonderful, feeling easy and relieved and just all over pert for the first time since that morning.

"You look like a fellow that has just had a bad tooth pulled," said Mr. Grey. "You are all over what was ailing you?"

I nodded. "I didn't mean to be rude. I was just— disappointed."

"Because you wanted to talk to me, and Susannah was there?"

"Yes, Sir."

"Well, she is not here now, Charlie. What was it you wanted to talk to me about?"

"Boxing lessons."

Mr. Grey clapped his hands. "Shuck your coat, Charlie, and step out into the sunshine. Professor Grey's course of instruction in the manly art is about to begin."

The next twenty minutes were among the most instructive of my life. For one thing, I learned that, try as I might, I could not land a blow on the agile person of Josiah Grey. I learned that losing one's temper is not conducive to accuracy, and that dropping one's left is an open invitation to disaster.

My nose was bleeding, I was soaked with sweat, and I was having the time of my life when the drumming of hoofbeats alerted us to the approach of a spanking yellow-wheeled rig come out from town.

"You go wash up at the pump, Charlie," said Mr. Grey. "We've got company."

The icy water felt shockingly good on my sweated face. I sluiced myself liberally, neck and arms and brow, then shook myself as dry as best I could and went jogging back to where the buggy had halted. I could hear a voice, loud, angry, but indistinct, and my curiosity spurred me into a lope. Even so, I got only the merest glimpse of Jock Moncreiff's crimson face before he whipped up his chestnut mare and went spinning on over the gravel.

"Wasn't that Mr. Moncreiff?" I said, by way of offering Mr. Grey an opening.

"Looked like him, didn't he?" replied Josiah Grey, with more than a tinge of sarcasm in his tone. Then he said, "I am sorry, Charlie. You were being a bit obvious, and I am getting a bit thin-skinned.

"Yes, that was himself."

"What was he yelling about?" I said.

Mr. Grey looked at me as if undecided how to respond. "You sure do plow right in with your questions, Boy. I had an aunt like that, Aunt Loretta. She was the most questioning woman that ever wore a bonnet. 'Where did you get that coat?' 'How much did it cost?' 'Did you write your mother?' 'How much are they paying you to teach those children?'

"I tell you, when that woman died they couldn't get her buried for nearly a week because she kept sitting up in her coffin and asking questions of the undertaker. That was seven years ago, and I doubt she has gone to glory yet. She is probably still quizzing St. Peter at the gates, just making sure the accommodations are tolerable."

"Sorry," I said. "I didn't mean to pry."

"Oh, well," he said, draping an arm across my shoulders, "I was always partial to Aunt Loretta. She was feisty as a rat terrier, and she kept on going till she was ninety-two. Curiosity may have killed the cat, but it is what kept old Aunty going. You, now, will probably live to be a hundred."

I let him run on, and I didn't interrupt. I knew he was just filling in the space till he'd made up his mind.

"Put on your coat, Charlie. It is getting coolish, and you don't want to go getting a chill or you won't be able to spar with me tomorrow."

"Can we have another lesson tomorrow?"

Mr. Grey nodded. "We'd better, or you are going to get yourself killed. You've got good wind, Charlie, and you have got grit. But that left hand of yours is a scandal."

I slipped into my coat and buttoned up against the nippy wind. "Will I be any good, do you think?"

"You will be as good as you are willing to be. I don't say that you will be able to stand up to Mr. John Lawrence Sullivan, but if you are willing to work and to train, you should be able to give a respectable account of yourself."

"Did you ever see John L.?"

"Once."

"What was he like?"

"Drunk."

"Oh."

Mr. Grey laughed. "I am sorry, Charlie. Perhaps I am being unfair. He was not so very drunk. I mean, he was standing up. And he is a mighty fighter. It is just that his views on people of color are the same as Mr. Moncreiff's."

"Is that what he was shouting about?"

"Very good, Charlie. Very good indeed. You show a Pinkerton persistence. R.P. himself could do no better." Mr. Grey struck a fighting pose and tapped me playfully on the jaw.

Without thinking, I leveled a left at his mid-section that resulted in a satisfying "Woof!" I don't know which of us was the more startled. I do know that my feet were having an argument with my head, but my head won and I did not bolt.

"Whew!" said Mr. Grey. "'The pupil wipes the master's eye'—or his breadbasket. That was well sent, Sir. You have the reflexive instinct."

"I—I didn't think," I said.

"Good. You may think before a fight, or after. When you are in it, just act and react. We will work on it."

"Tomorrow?"

"Every day. You have got the makings, Charlie Prescott. It is a pleasure to work with you."

I grinned, delighted, and turned to go.

"Oh, Charlie."

"Sir?"

"That was what Mr. Moncreiff and I were having words about."

I stared up at him. "He came by to yell at you for being colored?"

"Not exactly." Mr. Grey, with a rueful look, rubbed his jawbone with his knuckles. "It seems that Susannah has been a little too enthusiastic about school this term. He—ah, took exception to her arriving so early and lingering so late."

"You mean he thinks you—like her?"

"Something like that."

"Oh, for—"

"Careful, Charlie."

"Yes, Sir." I was having trouble digesting it. "But nobody could be that crazy. Sukey Moncreiff? That is the foolishest thing I ever heard of."

Mr. Grey smiled. "Of course it is. I mean, just because she is the prettiest girl in the whole Territory, and the sweetest singer, and the brightest... Why, Charlie, you look as though you have swallowed your Jew's harp sideways."

"It's not funny," I said. "She is nothing but a snippy old girl, and I think you should have given her father a crack in the snoot."

"I will keep that in mind, Charlie. I really will." Mr. Grey laughed. "Now you had better get along home, or Miss Clara will stop your rations."

"Yes, Sir."

"And remind her that she has a lesson tomorrow evening."

"Oh, she remembers."

"Better than some of my scholars, I daresay. Scoot, now. I will see you tomorrow."

I scooted, and in a far happier frame of mind than when I had entered the schoolhouse that morning. Mr. Grey and I were friends again, and I was learning to box. Life looked about as good as it had ever looked to me.

In the weeks that followed, spring seemed to hesitate over setting up camp on the Wind River range. But my days were all of a piece, and I liked the pattern. I could almost feel myself growing from day to day. The physical demands of training and sparring with Mr. Grey, and the mental stretching and flexing in the schoolroom kept me on the move from sunup to dark. I cannot recall another time when sleep came so easily or wrapped me so completely in quilted dreamlessness.

It was a good time for me, but it was in some ways a time of almost total absorption in myself. Oh, Father and Clara were there, and the Sheriff moved in and out of my days, but I had not much time to notice anyone. I neglected Jamie Sinclair, and even the lure of Morgan le Fay, his pretty little mare, was not so tempting as to keep me from my own pursuits. Sukey Moncreiff was less of a presence in the schoolroom, not that she ever missed a day. That was not her style. She was a scholar, I'd give her that. But she was no longer forward and no longer a nuisance. Whole days would slip by without my so much as noticing her. I counted it no loss.

My growing proficiency with my fists, and a new appetite for learning that pleased Mr. Grey and delighted Father, narrowed my days into a tight little circle. Even the search for the train robbers escaped my concern. I was more interested in my Indian club routine than in the dreary affairs that occupied older heads around me. But my aloofness was not to last.

One evening, as Father and I sat in congenial silence over the remains of a splendid raisin pie, Sheriff Finn came to call.

"Draw up a chair, Sheriff," Father said. "I think we can find a drop of coffee somewhere about the premises, and perhaps Charlie will yield to you in the matter of that last slice of pie?"

"Charlie?" said the Sheriff. "Who is Charlie?"

"Oh, you remember Charlie," my father said. "Charlie, say hello to Sheriff Finn."

I looked from one to the other, not certain if there was a joke a-foot.

"He does look familiar," said the Sheriff, forking up a mouthful. "I can't quite place him, but there is

something about the eyes that reminds me of a feller
that used to stop by my quarters to swap lies and scratch
old Blue back of the ears."

"That's him," Father said. "That's the same
Charlie."

The Sheriff shook his head. "Well, I couldn't swear
to it, Mr. Prescott. The Charlie I knew was not the sort
to let four or five whole days slide by without stopping
in to neighbor."

"I have been awful busy," I muttered.

"You see how it is, Sheriff," Father said. "He has
been busy."

"Humph." The Sheriff took a gulp of his coffee.
"Well, if I was ever to get so busy as to start neglectin'
my friends, I'd go off and have a talk with myself about
what kind of business I was in."

"I have been meaning to stop by," I said, feeling
just a little less impressed with my noble endeavors.

"I knowed a feller once, down in Carson. He was
always meanin' to write his wife and have her come out
and join him. He'd struck a mother lode and was
workin' like a one-man mule team just haulin' out ore
and turnin' it into money. Got so he wouldn't even
knock off of a Sunday to wash his shirt or mend his
britches. He was the most scarecrow lookin' feller I ever
laid eyes on. But rich. Yessir, he was rollin' in wealth.
Just rollin'. They used to call him the Silver Midas, but
he went around them parts lookin' like Lazarus at the
gate."

"Did he send for his wife?" asked Father.

"Well, he was meanin' to. That's what he always said. And I had no reason to doubt him. But the months piled on, and I never see no sign of a wife around his cabin. I used to stop out to his place of an evenin' to play checkers with him. He was a powerful checker player and a hard man to beat.

"Last game I played him, he cleaned the board in about a quarter of an hour. That very night I says to him, 'Jabez, why don't you knock off and take a run back East and see that little woman of yours?'

"'I'm meanin' to, Mr. Finn,' he says. 'I mean to take out another ton or two, and then I mean to buy me some store clothes and a train ticket and go fetch Louisa.'

"He had a tintype of her propped up against the tea caddy. She was a handsome woman, Mr. Prescott. Had them kinda doe eyes, y'know, and thick chestnut hair—leastways, he said it was chestnut—piled up high, the way them ladies wears it in the pictures in *The Police Gazette*.

"I says, 'If I was you, Jabez, I wouldn't waste no more time. I'd get back to that little woman on the next train out.'

"'I'm meanin' to, Mr. Finn,' he says. 'I'm meanin' to.'"

"And did he?"

"No, sir. Mineshaft fell in on him the next day. They talked about diggin' him out, but it would have been such a nation tough job that they give up on 'er and just stuck up a marker somewheres in the neighborhood of where they judged the body to be."

The Sheriff drained off his coffee. "His wife come into a sight of money, of course. Sold his claim, too. She took to travelin' and went off to England and It'ly and such like foreign places. She found herself one of these Eyetalian counts to help her spend the old man's money, and I guess he done his best. I hear he run through it pretty good, then left her for some New York nabob's hoss-faced daughter who had a hankerin' to call herself a countess. I just hope she could count better 'n old Jabez's pore little widder could. They say she died a pauper."

"It always amazes me, Sheriff," said Father, crossing his knife and fork on his plate, "it purely amazes me the way you can come up with these parables. So appropriate, too."

"We-ell," drawled the Sheriff, "I may not have prospered, Mr. Prescott, but I have led a colorful life. And I have kept my eyes and ears open. Seems to me that a chap can learn almost as much thataway as he can from settin' to a Harvard schoolmaster."

"Hem!" Father cleared his throat noisily. "Perhaps you had better get to the business that brought you here this evening."

"Yes, Sir," said the Sheriff, grinning wickedly. "I'm meanin' to."

I had been about to ask if I might be excused. I'd wanted to go upstairs and swing my clubs. But now I couldn't. I would not have dared.

"You recall a few weeks back when I mentioned a new rider out to Sinclair's place?"

"I do."

"Well, he wasn't around when I first went out to call, so I moseyed out there again on a pretext, and I got a good look at that feller. He is a hard case and no mistake. I could see straight off that he wasn't no drover. He was dressed like a dude, and just a glance at his hands would tell he never dug a posthole nor roped a steer in his life.

"When he seen me ride up, he ducked into the bunkhouse, and for a minute I thought he might be trying to dodge my acquaintance. But that was a mistake. He come out in about two shakes, and he was wearin' iron. It was the way he was wearin' it that gave me the fantods. He had one of them quick-fire rigs, you know what I mean?"

"No holster?"

"You called it. There was his Peacemaker, naked as a newborn possum and just danglin' from a stud in a slotted plate in his belt. All's he has to do is swivel that piece from his hip and start throwin' lead. I cal'clate he could loose two rounds before another man could clear leather. And from the way he was eyin' me, he wouldn't be any too proud to have a go at it."

"You could take him, Sheriff," I said.

"Why, Charlie, I thank you for your vote. But don't you go bettin' your wages on me. I have gone up against three fellers that was faster 'n me, and I expect I have just met the fourth."

"What happened to those other three, Sheriff?"

"Well, Charlie, two of 'em is dead, and one's a cripple. They was faster but they didn't shoot true. Maybe their barrels was bent."

Father laughed. "And maybe this rascal's gun's no better."

Sheriff Finn shook his head. "I dunno," he said. "You can't go countin' on a thing like that. One thing's certain. A man don't wear a quick-fire rig for poppin' jackrabbit. It is a killer's outfit, Mr. Prescott, and the side-winder packin' it has got killer's eyes."

"What on earth does Sinclair want with a hired gun?"

"My very question, Mr. Prescott. I asked him straight out why he put that soft-handed gunslinger on his payroll. The old man shoots daggers at me out from under them bushy eyebrows of his and says, 'Mr. Finn, I have little faith in public officials. When the next shipment goes out, I will have the satisfaction of knowing that there is a professional keeping watch over my interests.'"

"Umph," grunted Father. He eyed the Sheriff with mingled speculation and curiosity. "That was something of a slap, wouldn't you say?"

Sheriff Finn nodded. "It was. But I behaved myself. I says, 'Mr. Sinclair, I'd be obliged if you would introduce me to your new hand.'

"The old man took the bait and called his trained hound over. 'This is our Sheriff,' he says, like he had just bit into a green grape. 'This is Shad Clanton. Comes from down around San Antonio. That's Texas.'

"This Clanton and me, we kinda sniffed each other over like a couple of mongrels, and then I says, 'Your name may be Clanton, and maybe it ain't. And you may be from Texas, and maybe you ain't. But, Mister, if you was to come into my town wearin' that murderer's rig, you will wish to God you was back in Texas or wherever it was you was whelped.'

"'Here now, Sheriff,' says the old stager, 'what are you threatenin' Mr. Clanton for? He hasn't broken any laws.'

"'Not here, he ain't. Not yet,' I says, 'though I do not doubt but what I could find paper on him if I was to look through my Federal notices.'

"Then the gunslinger spoke up, not loud, mind you, but clear and steady.

"'I don't feel threatened, Mr. Sinclair,' he says. And he looks me up and down like I was somethin' you see in a sideshow at a circus. 'I may have seen sorrier specimens pinned to a badge in my time, but I cannot remember where that was, or when.'"

"That was slicing it thick," Father said.

"That is what I thought," said the Sheriff. "So I backhanded him. I think I may have broke his nose. Doc Dyer's out havin' a look at him. I expect we will hear all about it this evenin'."

"Sheriff," murmured Father, "you are a fearsome man."

"It comes with the badge," replied the Sheriff. He appraised his knobby knuckles with a shrewd eye. "'Course, I may not be one of these here scientific pugilists that dances around in a ring to entertain the quality. But when I go for to crack a man's jaw or break his nose or black his eye, I gen'rally succeed in crackin' that jaw or breakin' that nose or blackin' that eye."

"And you may succeed in stopping lead one of these days, if you aren't more careful."

Sheriff Finn grinned like a schoolboy. "Now that is what Mr. Sinclair's pet pistol said—or words to that effect. I cannot repeat his exact language in present company, but the sentiments was identical.

"I told him I would keep my back to the wall at all times."

"Do you think he will try to bushwack you, Sheriff?" I said, fear tightening my voice and sending it up an octave.

"Why, Charlie, there ain't no tellin'. In my trade, a man can't predict how the customers will behave. My suspicion is, an hombre that favors a quick-fire rig is a mite too jealous of his reputation to stoop to shootin' a broken down old lawman in the back. But then again, a busted nose changes a man's views quicker 'n free drinks on Election Day. I expect I will hear from this Clanton one way or another."

"Think maybe you ought to sign on a deputy?" Father asked, a worried look clouding his eyes.

"And what would I get? Shucks, Mr. Prescott, I will have enough to do just watchin' out for myself without havin' some tanglefooted freeloadin' incompetent runnin' at my heels."

Father shrugged. "You know best," he said.

"I know one thing. We can scratch Mr. Sinclair from our list of nominations."

"Seems so," Father said. "He certainly would not bring in outside talent to ride herd on his money if he meant to play a double game."

"Well," said the Sheriff, with what was supposed to be a subtle warning glance in my direction, "we can talk about this another day."

"This evening?"

"Suits me. I don't look for no broken-nosed gunslingers to be out and about tonight. I will be by after supper." The Sheriff settled his hat just so and gave a hitch to his britches. "Charlie, it has purely been a pleasure. I will tell Blue you was askin' for him."

"Tell him I will look in on him tomorrow, after school lets out," I said.

"I will do that. And don't you disappoint him. Blue has got his pride, you know." Sheriff Finn winked and was gone.

"He is not the only one," said Father, as the door closed on the departing Sheriff.

"Sir?"

"Oh, nothing important." Father looked at me as though he were studying my face, almost as if he meant to sketch me. Then he said, "Friendships are like fences, Charlie. They must be kept in good repair."

"Yes, Sir."

"Are you going upstairs to exercise with your Indian clubs?"

"Well, I—I wondered if you would like a game of checkers before dinner."

Father's smile was beautiful to see. "Get the board, Charlie," he said. "I will give you first move and still trim your whiskers."

It was as pleasant an evening as I had spent in a considerable while.

CHAPTER VII

I took Father's advice. It meant some shifts and adjustments, but I discovered that it was possible to continue my own pursuits and still keep my friendships in repair. And it was worth the effort.

Jamie Sinclair seemed especially pleased by this change. As a ranch boy, he knew better than most what loneliness is. Living more than ten miles from his nearest neighbor, Jamie had grown into a kind of self-sufficiency that sustained him during the long stretches between terms at school. I cannot imagine that his dour father was much company, however much the old man doted on his son.

Jamie's ma was even less society for him. A poor pale creature, she had never flourished in her husband's shadow, and after the birth of her only son she seemed to shrink into a perpetual invalid state. With hindsight, I am certain that the poor soul was unbalanced. It is no wonder. Her husband so thoroughly dominated her; she had no female companionship; there was nothing in her world to relieve her isolation—except Jamie, and he came into her life too late to prevent her slipping into the shade of alienation. She was not what my colleagues would call "insane," but she was out of touch with reality—harmless, sweet, wraithlike Alice Sinclair.

What I liked about Jamie, aside from his quiet competence and his evident pleasure in my company, was that he never pushed. He was a handsome, well-mannered boy with money in his pocket and an abiding sunniness of temper that made him the best of companions. Had he cared to, Jamie could easily have made himself the center of a wide circle of hangers-on—at least when school was in session. But he was above that. He went his own way, enjoying his own company when other society was denied him. He never stooped, he never ran after anyone. But let someone make the first tentative steps toward friendship, and Jamie would respond with a warmth and a frankness which, even then, I recognized as rare.

I was a better boy when I was with Jamie. He had a fundamental decency about him that was as much a part of his nature as the warmth and intelligence that lighted his honest blue eyes. And though he was older and bigger than me, a better scholar and a superior athlete, he never made me feel inferior.

There it is. That is the quality I have been struggling to identify, the trait I have so often looked for in others in vain. He never made me feel inferior.

So often what passes for friendship is mere tolerance, and unspoken agreement as to subordination. My several critics down the years have accused me of being aloof. Perhaps. I suspect, though, that I was so fortunate in the quality of my early friendships that I cannot now settle for mere sociability.

With Jamie there was friendship. We had a stretch of golden afternoons together that linger in my recollection as fresh and sweet as the prairie grasses after a summer shower. We roved far and free, trying our skills with rod and gun, or exploring the washes and gullies that, in spring, sent torrents of snowmelt tumbling down to freshen the watering holes so vital to the white-faced herds that cropped the greening range.

Sometimes, as on that perfect afternoon in early May, we were content to fling ourselves down on the sunwarmed earth and talk or not talk as the fancy took us. That day, Jamie was of a mind to talk, and I was happy to let him ramble.

"Father means to pack me off to boarding school next year. He said that if I work hard and apply myself, he will see me through Princeton."

"Where's Princeton?"

"It's in New Jersey."

New Jersey. I had heard of it, of course. We had been obliged to learn the states and their capitals, all 43 of them, to please Miss Sarah Louise Hathaway. But I will admit that whole months, years even, could pass without my ever thinking of New Jersey. Yet there was such a place. And there were people living there, and working and growing old and dying without giving so much as a passing thought to Wyoming and all the people living there, and working, and growing old, and dying without giving so much as a passing thought to New Jersey and all the people living there, and working, and growing old, and dying without... Well, once I let my mind run in that kind of groove, it is all up with me.

I was aware of Jamie's voice, but not a word did I hear. I was trying to picture New Jersey, trying to imagine a boy my age who at that very moment might be lying out on the ground and thinking about Wyoming. My thoughts were growing so complicated that they began to make me uneasy. I could not seem to corral them into a manageable bunch, and it was a welcome relief when Jamie flung a handful of grass at my head and demanded to know if I were listening.

"Um." I grunted and sat up. "You said you were going to New Jersey."

Jamie laughed. "I have already put in my time there and had just opened my law office in Cheyenne and begun to stump for Congress. Where have you been?"

I grinned sheepishly. "Still in New Jersey. Sorry, Jamie. I was woolgathering."

"Huh. You must have laid in about a hundred bales of it. I don't know why I bother trying to talk to you, Charlie. You aren't interested."

"Sure I am, Jamie. I think it is fine that you are going to go to Princeton. But what do you want to go to Congress for? I would never be happy living away from Wyoming."

"Oh, I'd always come back here," Jamie said. "This is home. But if I was to go to Congress, I could do a lot of good for Wyoming, make it a better place for my children to grow up in."

"Your children? You mean you are going to get married and all that stuff?"

"I hope so, Charlie. Aren't you?"

"Huh! Catch me! What do I want with some old wife bossing me around and having a conniption every time I wanted to smoke a seegar or go off a-huntin' or anything that's got some sense in it? Shoot, Jamie, if a feller has got a wife, he can't do anything. She is always after him to hang curtains or beat the carpets or buy her a new bonnet. Where would Sheriff Finn be if he had a wife? Where would Mr. Grey be?"

"I give up. Where would they be?"

"Hogtied. That's where. They couldn't go—" I broke off, remembering in time that Josiah Grey's business was not known to Jamie. "I mean, they would not be free to come and go."

"What do you want to be free to do, Charlie?"

"Everything. Why, suppose there was a gold strike, or maybe there was a war somewhere, or a chance to sign on board a clipper ship? What kind of show would I have if I had to bring home wages and set up nights discussing wallpaper patterns with some fussbudget female who could flat out faint if a darned old mouse was to scoot across the room?"

Jamie laughed and shook his head. "You sure have a low opinion of females, Charlie."

"That's all right, Jamie. You'll see. Some night you will want to sit up and play five-card stud with a bunch of senators, or the President, or somebody like that, and your wife'll say, 'You promised to take the children to the magic lantern show.'

"Where's your card game then, hey? What kind of life is that? There's the President waiting for you to cut the cards, and his servant says, 'Mr. President, Congressman Sinclair sends his regrets. He can't play poker with you tonight because he has to take his children to the magic lantern show.'

"Do you think the President is going to ask you over to play cards another time? Why, you would be lucky if he was to so much as say 'Howdy' when he passed by your pew of a Sunday."

"My career is ruined," murmured Jamie. "And it seemed so full of promise."

"You may laugh all you want to, Jamie Sinclair, but you just better remember that people want a Congressman that stands in solid with the Big Chief. It is men that do the voting, and real men are not going to vote for a Congressman that can't even be boss of his own house. Might as well send women to Congress and be done with it."

"I bet they will."

"Will what?"

"Send women to Congress."

"Have you been chewing on loco weed? Honestly, Jamie, for a levelheaded feller, you can come out with the craziest darned-fool notions I ever heard. Women in Congress? Can you imagine what a henhouse racket there would be? Why they would be making laws about planting forget-me-nots on the White House lawn, and maybe painting the White House pink or lavender or some such girl-baby color. Why, they would have the army wearing lace on their uniforms and put window boxes on all the battleships."

Jamie gave it up. I guessed that he knew I had him. Maybe it was the pink White House; maybe it was the window boxes. I am not certain. But he allowed that maybe the country was not quite ready for Congressladies just yet.

"And not for the next two hundred years," I said, nailing down my argument.

"You may be right, Charlie."

"Of course I am right. And if I was you, Jamie, and was serious about getting elected, I wouldn't go around talking such wild talk where folks could hear me."

"But you will vote for me, won't you, Charlie?"

"If you want. I am not sure I will be doing you any favor, but just so long as you don't go stumping for votes for women or anything crazy, I will mark my ballot for you."

"Fair enough. I promise I won't say anything crazy."

"Golly, Father's going to say something if I don't shove for home. He does not take it kindly when I come late to dinner."

"Race you to the Crossing!"

We were off like a pair of young pronghorns. Jamie was taller, of course and had longer legs, but I was able to give him a race. He reached the little wooden bridge only seconds before me.

"You are getting there, youngster," he said, blowing hard, and brushing the hair back out of his eyes. "I will have to start training if I mean to stay ahead of you."

"You'd better," I said, "for I mean to beat you before summer comes."

"Well, if I must be beat, I'd rather be beat by you than by anybody else. You are a good friend, Charlie. I enjoyed our talk today. Thank you."

That was Jamie. I never knew a politer boy, nor a nicer. I set out for home in the twilight chill, warmed by the friendship of an older, and I am afraid a better boy. I began to trot as the sky deepened to an inky blue. My appetite was never delicate, and now I had hot biscuits on my mind.

About a half mile from the edge of town, I opened up and began to lope, my breathing easy, a cool wind at my back. Perhaps if I'd been paying more notice, perhaps if I hadn't been dwelling on dinner, I might have avoided what happened next. But I doubt it. It was all so quick and unexpected.

I remember rounding a bend at a good clip, and suddenly a dark form exploded from the brush. Something hit me with the force of a locomotive. My feet went out from under me, and I hit the ground like a felled oak. When the stars and comets cleared away, I was flat on my back, with my wrists pinned, a pair of bony knees grinding into my biceps, and a leering, gap-toothed face looming large before my frightened eyes.

"Gotcha, ya little sonofabitch. Now I guess you will find out what comes of crossin' Rufus Jakes."

Rufe yanked me to my feet and cuffed me once or twice about the head. "This way, youngun. And don't you try nothin' or I will carve your ears off."

I believed him. I didn't try anything. I was so scared and my brain was so addled that I couldn't think of anything to try.

Rufe prodded me along with that Ozark toothpick of his, directing me up a low rise to where a shaggy evil-looking mule was hobbled. The brute eyed me with no very loving glance as we approached, and he made a try at biting my leg as Rufe boosted me up onto his bare back.

"Hee-hee! See that? If you don't behave y'self, I will feed you to old Samson. He has et his share of younguns and slow movers in his day, and he ain't too proud to make a meal of you."

Rufe loosed the hobbles and swung up behind me. His closeness, given his constitutional aversion to soap, was not pleasant. He jerked at Samson's iron mouth and urged him on through the scrub.

I judged we'd gone about three miles and a little bit when I saw smoke rising among the stunted trees. In a few minutes we reached a miserable little soddy dug into the side of a low bluff. Rufe let out a better than fair imitation of a whippoorwill. The door swung out, and there was Harney Jakes, ugly as ever, and looking uncommonly happy to see me.

"Hey, Rufe," he said. "You got 'im, huh?"

"I gen'rally git what I go fer. Stable Samson and come inside."

Harney sniggered as Rufe assisted me up the step with a middling hard thrust of his boot, and he hurried off to bed down the mule.

I think I never appreciated Clara's qualities as a housekeeper till I saw the inside of that wretched hut. Empty tins littered the dirt floor. A demi-john stood within easy reach of the lone chair, a lumpy cushioned

armchair that must have come over on the Mayflower—
or the Ark. Four bunks, little more than plank shelves,
were built into the walls, and I estimated that the ratty
old blankets had not had the benefit of a wash or an
airing since Columbus landed. A rope was strung the
length of the house, and a faded union suit was draped
over it for all the world like the corpse of a man that had
fallen on a fence just as he died of starvation.

Spiders' webs and grime combined to hold down
the amount of light admissible through the two small
windows, and there was an unmistakable essence of
mouse or suchlike livestock in the air. A coffeepot and a
scattering of tin ware decorated the splintery table.
From the scarcity of chairs I judged that the tenants
took their rations standing up.

"Home sweet home," said Rufe Jakes. "Purty, ain't
it? Not what you're used to, I expect, but it keeps the
rain off. Most of it."

"That you, Rufus?" A quavering voice floated out
from what proved to be a tiny pantry.

"Naw, it's Gen'ral Grant. Who in hell did ya think
it was, you old fool?"

Daddy Jakes, looking like a graveyard haunt, hobbled out, leaning heavily on a crudely fashioned crutch.
Rufe lit a smoky lamp and set it down on the cluttered
table. The old man's weasel eyes blinked rapidly for a
bit, then focused on me. A gloating smile widened his
sunken mouth.

"You fetched him," Daddy Jakes crowed. "Hot
damn, Rufus, you really done it."

"Looks like it, don't it? Now stir yourself, old man, fix us some grub."

"Harney got us a couple of rabbits."

"Well, fry 'em up, dammit. Anything left in the jug?"

The old man looked grieved. "Rufus, you know I wouldn't polish off the last o' your squeezin's."

"Not unless you was lookin' to have your throat cut, you gimpy old rummy." Rufe dropped his long frame into the chair and hoisted his jug. He held it up to his ear and sloshed it around. "You been at it, though, you old vulture. Ain't enough left to kill a toothache."

"Now, Rufe," the old man whined, "you can't begrudge your old pa a nip. Way my laig's been achin', I needed a little wettin' to ease the pain."

"I shoulda took your laig right off while I was at it," Rufe growled. "I would've, too, if I'd 'a knowed what a damned nuisance you was goin' to make of yourself."

"It ain't my fault, Rufus," protested Daddy Jakes, dropping some grease into his skillet. "By rights you should blame that no-'count Sheriff. He is the one that shot me."

"He should've aimed for your head," said Rufe, taking a pull at his jug. "Damned shame he didn't."

Mumbling and whining to himself, Daddy Jakes gave up on his bid for sympathy and devoted his attention to the unlucky rabbits. Harney came in and, evidently aware that it was no time to trouble Rufe, contented himself with glowering at me from his perch on one of the rumpled bunks.

Rufe tipped his jug to its zenith, swallowed passionately, set it down with a sour look and hauled himself up out of his chair. "God damn! There ain't nothin' worse than not enough."

"Maybe you-know-who will bring some o' that sippin' whiskey with him when he rides out tonight, Rufus."

"Shut your head, you miserable old skeleton. Where in hell's my rations? Do you mean to burn 'em up?" Rufus arranged the plates on the table with a good deal more noise than precision. "Come on, dish it out. And give a hunk to our guest of honor. Got to keep him fat and sassy."

"Didn't have but the one onion, Rufus," said the old man sorrowfully. "By rights there should be more onions."

"Tell you what," said Rufe, watching the old man fork out the charred and stringy chunks. "When we finish our business here, I will personally buy you a whole barrel of onions. How's that?"

"Hee-hee. That'll be fine, Rufe. I like that fine."

"And if you don't stop your everlastin' bellyachin', I will shove you head first into that barrel and use it for your coffin."

Rufe took up a plate. "Here, Harney. Eat up."

Harney grabbed his plate and set to with an enthusiasm unwarranted by the looks or the smell of the fare.

"You, kid." Rufus beckoned to me. "Come and git it."

I ventured to the table, took one look, and shook my head. "Not hungry," I said.

Rufus shrugged. "More for us," he said. "I guess you are used to better rations."

"And better company." The words were out before I thought, and Harney, with equal lack of forethought, reached out and fetched me a smack high up on the side of the head. And I, still not thinking, came back at him with a really pretty right hand that sent him sprawling.

"Whoo-ee!" cried Rufe Jakes, slapping his thigh and executing an impromptu jig. "Looky what we got here. Get out o' the way, Daddy, and mind the lamp chimbly. We gonna have us a shindy."

He yanked the astonished Harney to his feet, then collared the pair of us. "All right, you two hotheads. Let's see a real fight. And Harney, if you don't whup him, I will skin you alive and use your hide to patch my moccasins."

Harney snorted in contempt. "Huh! I guess if I can't whup this nigger-lover, I will have to start wearin' a skirt and playin' with doll babies."

Rufe dragged the table to one side, clearing an arena for Harney to work his bloody deeds in. Daddy Jakes, leaning on his crutch, took up a post near the cookstove and cackled in gleeful anticipation. "You bust him up good now, Harney."

Rufe took his seat of honor and guffawed as I struck a fighting stance. "Oooh-eee! Ain't that somethin'? Knock his block off, Harney."

Harney might have done just that, had his first blow landed. But he had no science. He swung mightily, but I leaned back, then fired a very satisfactory left hand to his ear as the impetus of his haymaker carried him into harm's way. I followed up with a smart right to his breastbone that seemed to cause Harney to reflect on the size of the job he had undertaken.

He stood there, fists at his sides, blinking and shaking his head. There could be no doubt that he was re-thinking his strategy.

"Rassle the sucker, Harney," advised Rufe, "if ye have the stomach for it."

Harney sprang for me, arms outstretched. With shameless pleasure, I sidestepped and leveled a perfectly lovely right hand into his belly. He dropped to all fours and retched horribly.

Rufe's booted foot shot out and caught the fallen Harney in the short ribs. "Get up, damn you! You are disgracin' the fam'ly."

This appeal to ancestral pride, coupled with the sharp inspiration of his brother's boot, served to rouse Harney to combat once more. But it was a forlorn hope. Harney was game, I'll give him that. But despite the instruction and abuse hurled at him from ringside, he just couldn't come it. I hit him when and where I pleased, and I confess that it did please me more than is fitting for a boy of Christian principles. I purely demolished Harney Jakes, and when even Rufus had to concede that Harney had had enough, I felt a surge of unholy glee mingled with relief. Glad as I was to have whipped Harney, I was arm-weary and winded, and I knew that, had he succeeded in closing with me, Harney would surely have realized his ambition.

I was scared, too. For it occurred to me that Rufe might take it unkindly that I had so thoroughly worn out

Harney. But I needn't have worried. Rufe's wrath was all directed at his younger brother.

"Git up and go on out to the well and wash your face, you miserable whelp. You are leakin' blood all over the floor."

"Why'nt you throw yourself down the well whilst ye're at it?" suggested Daddy Jakes. "I don't know when I have ever been so shamed. To think I would live to see a Jakes git whupped by a damned little Sunday School puppy—"

"Oh, shut your head, old man," growled Rufus. "Save it for breakfast."

Daddy Jakes subsided, muttering to himself and shaking his head over this sullying of the family honor.

Rufe now turned to me and eyed me appraisingly. "You done good, youngun. Who learned you to fight that way?"

"Mr. Grey," I said.

"The nigger? Humph. Well, he learnt ye good, I'll give him that. Old Harney will be wantin' his rations cut up for him for the next week or two, I reckon. That nigger sure is a caution."

"I thought you had reason to know that before now," I said.

"Looky here, boy, don't go gettin' feisty with me. I ain't Harney. You give me any more lip and I just might take a notion to have a look at your liver."

The thought of Rufe's Ozark toothpick was intimidating, but my blood was up. "You just do that," I said, "and you will have Sheriff Finn coming down on you like the walls of Jericho."

Rufe shook his head, laughing. "You are a sandy little sucker and no mistake. But you better know that Finn don't scare me any. I have gunned down a dozen sheriffs in my day, as good or better than what Finn is. It wouldn't grieve me none to shoot him, too."

"In the back?"

"Back or front, I ain't partic'lar. I will get to Finn one of these days. Right now I got other business to tend to."

"Such as?"

"God damn, boy! I never see the beat of you for sass. Your pa oughta take a stick to you and learn you manners."

"Likely he will take a stick to you when he finds out you have run off with me. What did you bring me here for anyway? I want to go home. I want—"

"Hold up! Just hold up, now," Rufe commanded. "I ain't concerned with what you want. I got fish of my own to fry. You put a check rein on that mouth o' yours and behave yourself. You will be goin' home soon enough, I reckon. I don't fancy your company anyway. You are a whole lot too mouthy for your size. I will be as glad to be shut of you as you will be to be shut of me, I guess. So do as I tell you, and there won't be no bones broken. At least, none o' your bones anyway."

At this juncture Harney came sidling in, looking about as miserable as a stray dog in a sleet storm. Anyone could see that his one hope was to attract no notice, but it was not Harney's lucky day.

"What kept you?" Rufe demanded. "You fall down the well?"

"No loss if he did drown," muttered Daddy Jakes as he hobbled to the stove for coffee.

"Get down the writin' things, Harney," said Rufe. "And then get out o' my sight. Your face ain't nothin' to look at right after a man has et."

Poor Harney, self-pity plain on his battered face, rummaged around on a crowded shelf and reached down a sheet of foolscap and a thick carpenter's pencil. "I got 'em, Rufe," he said, in a naked bid for approval.

Rufe was not impressed. "Get out o' my sight," he said. "Go to bed. Or go hang yourself."

Harney, with a woebegone look, shuffled off to the far side of the room and flung himself down on his bunk. He turned his face to the wall, drew a blanket up over his head, and pretended to go to sleep.

Rufe cleared a place on the plank table, then beckoned to me. "I want you to write a letter, boy," he said. "You write what I tell you, and write it good so's your pa can read it right off with no misunderstandin'."

"S'pose I don't?"

"Then I slice off one of your ears and send that to your pa instead."

I knew one thing. Rufe was not too good to do it. So I licked the point of the pencil and said, "What do you want me to write?"

"You write to your pa and you tell him you are bein' held pris'ner. If he wants you back, he is to send $500 cash by way of that nigger schoolmarm by noon t'morra. The nigger is to come alone. Any tricks, and your pa will be a child short. You got that?"

I nodded.

"Then write it."

As I formed my letters, I glanced up to see Rufe peering over my shoulder. "What's that say so far?" he demanded, nudging my arm with a grimy knuckle.

"'Dear Father, I am being held prisoner at the sod house near Olson's place.'"

"That all? You are a slow writer, boy.

"This pencil is right down awkward."

"Never mind the pencil. Just get to writin'. That message has got to go out tonight."

"How come Mr. Grey has to bring the money?"

"Don't you worry your head about Mr. Grey. I got plans for Mr. Grey. You just better hope he don't turn rabbit on you and run off."

I resumed writing. "Rufe Jakes says to tell Mr. Grey to bring $500 here by noon tomorrow, if you want to see me alive. Tell Mr. Grey, '*Hanc cave. Hodie mihi, tibi cras.*"

"You done?"

"Just have to sign my name." I did that and handed the sheet to Rufe. I held my breath and tried to look unconcerned as he stared at the letter.

"You write a poor hand, boy."

"So Mr. Grey says."

"Well, I hope for your sake your pa c'n read it. Lord knows I can't."

That was what I had counted on. "Want me to read it back to you?"

"I don't need no help from you." Rufe strode over to the bunk and snaked the blanket off Harney. "Git up, you miserable little shoat."

Harney knew better than to pretend drowsiness; he swung his feet to the floor.

"Read this," said Rufe, thrusting the letter at him. My heart dropped into my boots.

Harney knit his beetling brows and, with a stubby finger for a pointer, laboriously spelled out the first two lines. I closed my eyes and tried to pray.

"'Tell Mr. Grey,' droned Harney, 'tell Mr. Grey don't turn rabbit and run. Love. Charlie.'"

I opened my eyes in relief and disbelief. Harney couldn't read it either. But he had been listening, and he could remember.

"You read tolerable slow, boy," growled Rufe, swiping the paper from Harney's hand. "Couldn't that nigger learn you no better?"

Harney might have pointed out that Rufe could not read at all, but Harney was only dull, not simple. He had a keen sense of self-preservation.

"That was good you put it in about turnin' rabbit," Rufe said, folding the coarse paper and sealing it in a thick envelope. "That'll fetch him quicker'n anything."

"How are you going to get that letter to my father?"

"You are a nosy child and no mistake," said Rufe. "S'pose you jist lay yourself down on that other bunk and leave the mail to me, hey?"

I shrugged and did as I was told.

"Harney, tie him down. We don't want him to go wanderin' off. He might get lost in the dark."

Harney went about his work with a kind of sullen zest, binding my wrists together and lashing them to the bedpost.

"All right, now. You scutters get to sleep." Rufe said. "Don't let me hear no noise out of you between this and sunup."

I think I slept. Uncomfortable as I was, I must have dozed. Once, I remember, I waked briefly and heard voices talking low. My brain wasn't working right; I seemed to be swimming underwater, trying desperately to surface. I heard Rufe say, "Keep your voice down, dammit."

And another voice, a voice I knew but could not place, replied, "I still say you were a fool to grab the boy."

And then I was drowned in sleep.

When I woke again, I woke in utter terror. My eyes were streaming, my body was racked with coughing, and through a mist of tears and smoke, I saw Harney Jakes bending over me with a sheath knife in his hand.

I tried to cry out, to twist and kick Harney away. But he pinned me with his forearm and said, "Hold still!"

Quick as thought, he slashed through my bonds and dragged me out of the bed. Rufe Jakes, a gigantic shadow in the smoke, cursed and coughed as he shoved Harney and me through the door and out into the early morning light. We stumbled into the dooryard, and I fell full length on the dew-damped grass, my chest heaving, my lungs wheezing like leaky bellows. I looked back over my shoulder to see Old Daddy Jakes come hobbling through the rolling smoke, clutching at his ropey throat with a clawlike hand. Close at his heels came Rufe, buckling on his gunbelt as he stumbled into the blessed air.

"Good morning, Rufus," called a voice seemingly from out of the dawn-dappled sky.

I looked up and there, leaning against the chimney, smiling and chipper as a bluejay, stood Josiah Grey, his Winchester resting idly on his right shoulder.

Rufe Jakes cleared leather and got off a round. I saw Mr. Grey's hat whipped from his head as if by an unseen hand.

Mr. Grey lowered his rifle. "Good-bye, Rufus," he said, and he fired from the hip.

The slug tore into Rufe's belly, spinning him halfway around. He let out a wild cry, clutched at the crimson stain spreading over his shirtfront, went down hard, and died.

"Ye killed him, ye goddam nigger! Ye killed my boy!" screeched Daddy Jakes, his evil old face contorted in rage.

"I meant to," said Mr. Grey. "And I shall serve you the same way if you oblige me to. Just sit yourself down, Mr. Jakes; you, too, Harney, unless you mean to try to outrun a bullet."

Mr. Grey removed his broadcloth coat from the stovepipe, turned and pigeon-toed down the slight incline of the roof. He came around front, still cradling his Winchester, his coat draped over his arm.

"How are you, Charlie?" he said.

"Finer than frog hair," I said. "You're early."

"I try to be prompt. I hate to keep folks waiting." He strode over to Harney and Daddy Jakes and stood looking down at them. Harney seemed dazed. His ordinarily pasty face was paler still, and his eyes didn't seem to focus. The old man, his wattles turkey red, was just boiling, but he kept his tongue in check. The sight of Rufe's corpse not ten yards off was sufficient to inspire a prudent silence.

"Mr. Jakes," said Josiah Grey, "I noticed a mule stabled out back. I believe that a wise man would keep on riding till that mule gave out. I believe that now is the time to get started."

The old man straggled to his feet. "Come on, Harney," he said.

The look on Harney's face was too much for me. "Mr. Grey," I said.

"What is it, Charlie?"

"Don't make Harney go."

Mr. Grey frowned. "I am not making him go, Charlie. His father—"

"But Harney doesn't belong with him. He's not trash, not deep down. He—he cut me loose this morning."

Josiah Grey called out, "Mr. Jakes!"

"Well, what now?" Daddy Jakes turned back with a look that would have poisoned a well.

"The boy does not have to go with you, if he is of a mind to stay."

"What do you mean, not have to go? He's my boy, ain't he? Don't I need him to fetch and carry, and mebbe earn a bit o' money for my keep?" The old vulture shook his fist at Mr. Grey. "Don't you try to take my boy from me, or I will have the law on you."

Harney stood halfway between his scarecrow father and Mr. Grey, fear and hope contending on his poor dullard's face.

"You come along now, Harney. You got to help your poor old pa now. Rufe's gone, and you are all I got to keep me from starvin'."

Harney started draggin his feet after his father.

"Just a minute, Mr. Jakes." Josiah took a step forward. "If I were to supply you with some money—"

"You upstart nigger!" The old man fairly shrieked in his fury. "Your people may have been bought and sold, but I will be damned to everlastin' Hell before I let that happen to a Jakes. We are white men. And not all the books nor all the schoolin' in the nation will ever let you say as much.

"Harney, you git along now, afore I take my whip to ye. C'mon now, boy. I want us out of this nigger-lovin' territory."

I plucked at Mr. Grey's sleeve, but he shook his head. "It's no use, Charlie. The law is on his side in this. I handled it badly. If I'd had time to think, I might have found a way. I should never have offered him money."

"You tried," I said.

"So did you."

Well, there was comfort in that, but not much. I can still see the hopeless look that Harney Jakes turned on me as he trudged along after his derelict father. I like to think that things turned out well for Harney, that despite his origins and his upbringing, that spark of goodness that prompted him to cut me loose did not burn out. But I do not know, for since that morning I never saw nor heard of Harney Jakes again.

CHAPTER VIII

Father was that glad to see me that I'd have been willing to get myself kidnapped about once a month, just so long as I could arrange for my safe return. Clara fussed over me and ordered me into a hot bath, even though Saturday was whole days away.

"You been hangin' around Jakeses," she said. "No tellin' what kind of vermin you might have picked up. It wouldn't surprise me if you was come down with the mange."

The Sheriff came by to say howdy. He had to allow that Josiah Grey had done well. "Covering the chimbley is a boss dodge," he said. "I have used that more 'n once myself. But I didn't think there was a Pinkerton with sense enough to try it.

"'Course," he added, "he took a long chance with you in there. S'pose you was to have suffocated. Where'd he be then? Shopping for a tombstone, more 'n likely."

"What would you have done, Sheriff?" asked Father.

Sheriff Finn scratched his tawny thatch. "Hard t' say, Mr. Prescott. I'd have to look the place over, calc'late the odds, and then—" a grin spread over his good-humored face. "And then I guess I'd a-clumb up on the roof and draped my coat over the chimbly."

It pleased me no end to hear Sheriff Finn say that, and it seemed to please Mr. Grey, too, when I told him of it.

"Mr. Finn is a fair man," allowed Mr. Grey. "I know he would have preferred to take charge of your rescue himself. It went down hard with him when your father pointed out that there was no choice, that I had to be the one to go."

Mr. Grey smiled at the recollection. "It was plain to see that the Sheriff's confidence in my ability was, well, limited."

"I guess the Sheriff hasn't had much experience with detectives who speak Latin," I said.

Josiah Grey allowed that it could be so. Then he said, "Speaking of Latin, Charles, I appreciated your attempt to warn me, superfluous as it may have been. But I do wish you would pay closer attention to the niceties of the language."

"Sir?"

"You wrote *hanc* when you should have said *hunc*. Masculine, Charlie. 'Beware of him,' not 'her.' I might have been misled into believing that there was a lady waiting in ambush."

I felt deflated. It had seemed to me a bold stroke to add a warning in the classical tongue. Had Harney been a scholar, it could have cost me an ear, or at least a cuffing.

"That '*hodie mihi, tibi cras*' was a nice touch, though," Mr. Grey added. "I was, of course, aware that the unlamented Rufus had not singled me out from anything like affection. Still, it was good of you to be concerned for my safety when you yourself were *in extremis*. You must have been pretty scared."

I nodded. "You bet I was. Rufe Jakes is—was—meaner than a grizzly with the toothache. I wasn't what you would call comfortable the whole while."

"I can well believe it. And yet you cared enough to try to warn me. It is not a thing I will soon forget." Mr. Grey squeezed my shoulder. "I am certainly lucky in my friendships, Charlie. A man can't ask for much more."

It puffed me up considerably to hear that, but still I resolved to pay closer attention to number, gender and case.

"Mr. Grey," I said, "Who was it brought the note to Father?"

"I don't know, Charles. Whoever it was just wrapped it around a stone and flung it through the parlor window. Clara was that put out about it that she ran out into the street after him."

"Clara did that?"

"You didn't expect her to have the vapors, did you? Clara?" Mr. Grey shook his head and laughed. "I would rather stand up to any quantity of Jakeses than face Clara in her wrath.

"Whoever it was moved pretty lively, though. Clara did not get so much as a glimpse of him. I expect it was Harney."

"I don't think so. Harney was asleep before I was. At least I think he was asleep. He wasn't feeling any too grand."

"Um. That's right. You did thump him pretty thoroughly, didn't you?"

"I almost wish I hadn't," I said. "I feel bad about Harney, Sir. I purely hate to think of him off somewhere with that no-account father of his."

Mr. Grey smiled. "Hard to hate someone after you've whipped him, isn't it, Charlie?"

"Yes, Sir."

"But you did what you had to do. I am just glad that our lessons were not wasted on you. Did you remember to keep that right foot planted?"

"I think so. Truth is, I was so busy I didn't have time to think about it. I cut Harney up pretty badly."

Mr. Grey sighed. "Well, in a better world there won't be any fighting. But so long as you have to live in this one, it seems the better part of wisdom to hope for peace but be ready for war.

"But if Harney was laid up, as you say, who could have been the bearer of that message. Not the old man, surely. He couldn't move fast enough. Do you think Rufe—?"

"Wait! No, not Rufe. I don't think he would have left. He—he was expecting someone, someone who would be bringing along some whiskey. And someone did come. At least, I think so. I remember I woke up, or half-woke, just for a minute, and I heard someone, not a Jakes, talking to Rufe."

"Who was it Charlie? Did you recognize him?"

I shook my head. "I didn't see him. I heard his voice. Or I think I did. And I remember thinking that I knew the voice. And then I fell asleep."

"But you cannot tell now whose voice it was?"

"No, Sir. It—it slips away when I start to remember it."

"Well, it may not matter anyway. But if it should come to you, I would be mighty interested to know." Mr. Grey ended our conversation with offhand cheerfulness, but I could see that he attached considerable importance to the identity of Rufe Jakes's late-night caller. So, of course, I resolved to make myself remember. And of course I could not. I did not know then what I know now: that memory is like a recalcitrant child who will not come when called, but who will, if let alone, draw gradually nearer until he is within arm's reach.

It helped, certainly, to return to the familiar round of days—to school, and sparring with Mr. Grey, and helping Father in the shop, and going fishing or wildflowering with Jamie. Spring had definitely established residence: streams were swollen, and trout lurked in the shallow pools. Just at dawn I'd often hear the soft warble of the mountain bluebird or the loud flutelike call of the meadow lark celebrating the start of another day. The slopes and plains fairly swarmed with life; my skies were thronged with migratory flocks, and I was thrilled to hear great flights of geese calling overhead night and day.

Jamie and I were great collectors. Arrowheads, rocks, pelts and skeletons, feathers, eggs and nests were all our quarry, and we were adept at shinning trees or stealing through the waving prairie grasses to purloin still another specimen for our respective museums.

One bright Saturday afternoon, a week or so after my enforced sojourn among the Jakeses, Jamie and I kept a rendezvous at the edge of town and sallied forth to a scraggly copse where a kingbird had set up house-keeping. We meant to see if the mother had laid her eggs yet, and to help ourselves to one apiece if she had.

Jamie led the way through the thicket. He was a good companion on the trail. He saw things. And he was clever at finding the quickest way through a bad place. He was a regular Kit Carson, or so I thought until he let go the limber branch he was holding back and caught me solidly on the nose, raising a welt and making my eyes water shamefully.

"Jemminy Christmas!"

"Sh!"

"Oh, 'sh!' yourself, Jamie," I groused. "That hurt. What'd you let it go for anyway? Trying to blind a person?"

"Sorry," whispered Jamie. He tugged me by the sleeve and said, "Look there, Charlie."

My eyes were still leaking, and I wasn't much taken with Jamie's notion of an apology, but I stepped along and peered through an opening in the brush. About five rods up ahead I could make out a familiar figure running in our direction.

"Sukey!" I exclaimed. "What in time is she doing 'way off here?"

"I dunno," whispered Jamie. "Be still. Don't let her see us."

We scrunched down low and watched as Susannah Moncreiff came flying up the grassy slope. She could run; I had to admit it. And I suppose if I had not been so biased against anything in petticoats, I'd have conceded that she made a handsome picture with her fair hair flying loose in the glinting sunlight and the way her ripening figure was moulded by the action of the impertinent wind.

Sukey ran right by us, so close that I could have reached out and tapped her with my fish pole, if I'd had my fish pole with me. Jamie and I raised up a bit to get a clearer view. We saw her halt before a rheumatic looking apple tree that had given up long ago. Woodpeckers, worms and weather had pretty much had their way with that tree, and I judged that one kick of a lame mule would have made kindling of it. Sukey looked around hastily, then drew something from the bosom of her dress and thrust it into a hole in the tree.

"What in time—?"

Jamie silenced me with an elbow. He had the sharpest elbows of any boy I ever knew. Sukey took another quick look around, then went flying off towards home.

"Is it all right to breathe now?" I said.

Jamie grinned. "If you want to fight with Sukey, it's fine with me. I have no stomach for it myself, thanks all the same. Let's go look."

As usual, Jamie outlegged me. When I caught up with him, he was holding a folded sheet of paper in his hand and waving it under his nose. "Smells nice," he said. "Want a sniff?"

"I can smell it from here," I said, making a face. "You going to read it?"

Jamie looked thoughtful. "I'm not sure," he said.

That was a good sign. For a boy like Jamie, 'not sure' is practically the same thing as surrender. As for me, I wasn't concerned about the fine points. I just wanted to know what old Sukey was up to, and so long as I was not plainly breaking any Federal statutes, I could find a way to ease my conscience later. My conscience always did run about a half hour slow.

"The way I look at it," Jamie was saying, tapping the folded sheet against pursed lips, "it is not as if we were tampering with the mails. Because if this were an actual letter, of course, I—"

While he was working on his justification, I just took the paper from his hand, opened it, and read, "'Eight o'clock. The springhouse.'"

Looking back, I know I should have been too proud to read it. I know I should never have so much as glanced at it. And I wish I hadn't. But there it is. I was consumed with curiosity, and the question of morality did not surface. I was not, I am sorry to say, a model boy.

"I wonder who this is for," Jamie said, his own conscience apparently still under anesthesia. "You don't
suppose Susannah has a beau?"

"I would sooner kiss a hoptoad myself," I said.
"But what else can it be? Some sucker has sure enough
gone sweet on Sukey, and she has agreed to meet him by
moonlight."

"It is just like Romeo and Juliet," said Jamie.

"Hah! I can imagine what this Romeo looks like.
And I have already seen Juliet. Shakespeare must be
spinning in his grave. And I guess Old Man Moncreiff
would be spinning, too, if he knew what his pudding-
faced gal was up to."

"You aren't going to tell him, are you, Charlie?"

"Me? Tell Old Man Moncreiff? What are you
thinking about, Jamie? He would really thank me, now
wouldn't he? He would say, 'I am grateful to you,
Charlie. I think I will disinherit that ungrateful child and
make you my heir.'

"In a pig's eye! The last thing you ever want to do
with these nabobs is to be the one that tells 'em anything that is not just right and pleasant. If I was to tell
him that the price of beef is going up, or that all his
investments were doubling, or that we will have sunshine for the church social, why, I would be in clover.
But I would not be the one to bring him any bad news. I
would rather walk into Robbers' Roost with nothing but
my catapult and a Barlow knife than bring bad news to
Old Man Moncreiff.

"Besides, I think you and I should investigate this business and see if we can't maybe have a little fun with Miss Sukey Juliet Moncreiff."

"What d'you mean, Charlie?"

"I mean we have got to be at the springhouse by eight o'clock."

Right after supper, I pleaded a headache and was excused to go to my room. Clara was certain that I needed a tonic, but Father allowed we could afford to wait a day or two to see if the symptoms persisted. I was grateful to Father. That tonic was about as foul a potion as ever slid over my teeth. Clara swore by it. I swore at it. I don't know what was in it, and I don't want to know. But if there is any truth to the notion that equates unpleasantness with effectiveness, that stuff should have been able to cure anything from croup to consumption.

It was taking a considerable chance to go sliding out while the family was still awake, but it was a risk I had to take. I eased the window up and clambered out onto the sloping porch roof. Whoever had planted that box elder next to the house did not know boys. It made a most convenient natural ladder, and in two shakes I was on solid ground and flying crosslots like a lawyer racing a preacher to the bedside of a dying miser.

I was about winded when I reached Moncreiff's place, and I had a stitch in my side that didn't seem to want to quit. I judged that I had time enough, so I dropped down on the grass to blow off steam and cool down. My heart was hammering in my ears, and I was pretty well sweated. I believed that I could have drunk about five gallons of water, and I was breathing so hard that I was afraid I could be heard a mile off. But I steadied down gradually, and my breath began to come easier. I lay back and let the pounding in my head die away as I stared up into the flocks of stars that ranged the boundless sky.

I always liked to look up at the stars, but I never looked too long. Feelings would come over me that even now I cannot express or explain. I think I can understand how ancient people found their gods among the stars.

Night deepened. It was so still that every sound seemed eerily loud and distinct. I have heard farm folks protest that they could actually hear the corn grow. I believe it. It seemed to me that, as my breathing returned to normal, all my senses were wholly alive and almost supernaturally alert. The night air smelt green, if you know what I mean, and from miles away I could hear the mindless persistent barking of a dog that was unhappy about something, and the rising and falling of the puffing chug of an engine hauling its cars up the long valley to Old Man Moncreiff's mines. Closer to hand, a horned owl asked to know who I was, and nighthawks, emitting their peculiar tinny peeps, swooped low in their tireless search for dinner. In another minute, I could well have fallen asleep.

But then I heard the crunch of pebbles underfoot. I sat bolt upright, and let out a short sharp whistle. Sure enough, it was Jamie. He whistled right back, and in no time at all he hove into view, silhouetted on the top of a little low rise backed by a coppery three-quarter moon.

"Jamie," I hissed. "Over here."

He dropped into a crouch and scurried over to where I sat. "Any sign of her?" he asked.

"Not yet. Talk low. We got to get closer to the springhouse, and we can't risk being heard. Follow me."

"I don't know, Charlie," Jamie said, sitting down before me on the grass. "I've been thinking—"

I was afraid of that. The whole trouble with a boy like Jamie is, he will think.

"Listen, Jamie," I said, struggling to keep to whisper, "we got no time for thinking. It must be eight o'clock by now. If our fathers find out we skinned out we will most likely get a hiding, or at least a jawing. What is the point of going to all the trouble to get here, and then just give it up?"

"I just don't feel right about it, Charlie. It—it's low-down, and it isn't decent."

"Holy Moses, Jamie! You'd think we were planning to rob a church or something. All we want to do is—"

"Sh!"

Just as Jamie clutched my arm, I heard it. Someone was walking in our direction, someone who was taking no pains to avoid being seen. We heard the heavy tread of booted feet on gravel and the whispering sound of someone brushing through tall grass. Then the steps halted, and for a terrible moment Jamie and I crouched in breathless dread. Then, softly on the cool night air, there rose a melodious whistling, a tune that I immediately knew.

Off to our right, a latch rattled, a door swung wide, spilling a ray of light into the yard. A lithe white-clad figure slipped through the doorway, then all was dark again. The booted steps resumed, moving toward the springhouse, barely discernible in the dim starshine.

Cautiously, I reached out and found Jamie's shoulder. "Let's get out of here," I said.

"But I thought—"

"You were right, Jamie. You were right all along. Come on. We got no business here."

Slowly at first, we retreated, keeping to the edge of the gravel roadway so as to make no sound. Then, when we had put some distance between ourselves and the springhouse, I began to trot, and Jamie, like the good and loyal fellow he was, picked up the pace and trotted alongside me till we reached the edge of town.

In unspoken agreement, we halted in the shadow of the livery stable, knowing that we had behaved like fools, knowing that somehow we had got to get home without being seen.

"Who do you think it was, Charlie?" Jamie said.

"Got no idea," I said. But I lied. I knew who it was. I just didn't want to think about it, not then. I needed time and a quiet place in which to sort it out.

"Well, I guess we'd better get going, Charlie. Hope you make it without getting caught."

"You too, Jamie."

We were about to drift off on our separate guilty ways when the approach of a rider caused us to duck back into the shadows and wait. A flashy paint horse went high-stepping past, its rider sitting tall and loose in the saddle. He went right on by us, not noticing, his gaze fixed straight ahead.

"Lordy," I said. "I would trade my teeth for that horse."

"That's Shad Clanton," Jamie said. "He works for my father."

"The gunfighter?"

"Well, Father says he is a private guard." Jamie's tone lacked conviction. I guess he knew it, too, for he added in a stronger voice, "Father only means to keep him on till these robberies have been stopped."

I grunted. "Sheriff Finn does not take kindly to your Mr. Clanton. In fact, he about fractured his face for him."

Jamie nodded. "Father was pretty put out about that. He was that mad, I thought he—"

"Oh, Lord, Jamie!"

"What?"

"I bet Clanton's going for the Sheriff. I got to warn him, Jamie. That Clanton'll gun him down before the Sheriff even knows he's in town."

I took off at a dead run, and Jamie lit out after me. I took the back alley route, and for once in my life I outran Jamie Sinclair. My legs were churning and my heels were smoking. I must have scared the liver out of five or six cats, and the one I stepped on scared more than that out of me, but there was no time to swap knives or change linen.

I came to a sliding halt at the rear of the jailhouse, ducked down the side lane, and rapped hard on the window. The light went out, and I knew that the Sheriff was playing it foxy. If there happened to be a hardcase with a grudge to settle come rapping on his window-pane, Sheriff Finn was not going to make the work easy for him.

I stood there, shifting from foot-to-foot, waiting for the sash to rise when the weight of a hand fell on my nape and a familiar voice boomed out, "What in the hell are you two mavericks doing out here this time o' night?"

Well, I was all scared and glad at once, but I had to get my face cards up in a hurry, so I just blurted out, "Shad Clanton's riding in, Sheriff. I come to warn you."

All he said was, "I owe you, Charlie. Go home now."

And he was gone.

"Sweet Jesus, Jamie," I said. "There is going to be a shooting."

"You going home?"

"Not likely. You?"

"I'm staying," Jamie said.

We powwowed for a bit over the ideal vantage point, and we concluded that our best bet was the jail-house roof. But I'd hardly got a leg up on the lightning rod when we heard a cry in the street.

"You, Finn!"

"It's Clanton," Jamie said, his voice cracking with the excitement.

"Oh, damn, Jamie! We're going to miss it."

"Come out, Finn! Come on out here and die!" Clanton's voice was harsh and raspy as a crow's, and I could feel a cold hand closing around my bowels.

"It's early days to speak of dyin', Shad." The Sheriff's voice sounded steady and clear. "But if it is shooting you are after, I mean to oblige you."

"Well, come on then. I ain't a man to stand waitin'."

"Just cool your liver, Shad. I got you lined up in my sights, and this here Sharps has got a mighty touchy trigger. If you was to make a sudden move—"

"I was lookin' for fair play," Clanton said. "You wouldn't throw down on a man before he has had a chance to clear leather."

"You got no leather to clear, Shad. All I am doing is making sure I get through this door with a whole skin. When I make the street, I will drop the rifle and you c'n try your luck if you've a mind to."

"Fair enough."

"Stand clear, then, and keep them hands where I c'n see 'em."

We could hear the light clatter of the latch and the slow creaking of the jailhouse door.

"Come on, Charlie." Jamie tugged at my sleeve. "We can't see a thing from here."

"Let's get behind the horse trough in front of Cassidy's. Keep low, and we will run for it."

Bent almost double, Jamie and I fled the shelter of the alley and darted into the shadowed street. I was dimly aware of a scuffle of shoes and boots as the few folks abroad that night sought safety and a fair lookout from which to observe the killing, since there was killing to be done and it was not up to them to try to stop it. Certainly everyone was too preoccupied to notice a pair of young fools hunched down behind the trough, lighted though it was by the muted glow from Cassidy's frosted gilt-lettered window.

Jamie and I peered over the edge of the trough just in time to make out Sheriff Finn coming through the door. The barrel of his rifle gave off a dull gleam in the uncertain light.

"You just back off now, Shad, and give me room, or I will put a hole in you on principle."

"Take all the room you like," Clanton said. He backed up, his arms out, his hands well clear of his belt.

The Sheriff never took his eyes off Clanton. He moved deliberately, his rifle leveled across his forearm and trained on Clanton's belly. He halted in the middle of the street, his back to Jamie and me. "All right, Shad," he said. "I mean to drop my rifle now. When I do—"

Shad Clanton dropped to a crouch. His right hand slapped at the butt of his gun and he got off the first round. I saw Sheriff Finn pitch to the ground and roll over. Clanton fired again, and again.

Then the Sheriff, on his belly in the dust, snaked out his weapon and fired. I saw the spurt of orange flame, saw Shad Clanton straighten, heard his pistol fire a last time as his legs buckled under him, and I cried out as he crumpled and fell.

Sheriff Finn got to his feet and slapped the dust from his clothes with his hat. He holstered the Colt, tugged on his hat, and strode over to where Shad Clanton lay. With his booted foot for a lever, he turned the body face up. He stood staring down at the man he'd killed, then stooped and retrieved Clanton's gun and the belt with the quickfire rig.

People began to pour into the street to get a look at Clanton now that he was good and dead. Sheriff Finn shouldered his way through the crowd, ignoring their plaudits, and headed back to his quarters.

"God A'mighty, Jamie. He did it. He got Clanton and he ain't even nicked. Did you ever see such shootin' in all your life?"

But Jamie didn't answer. He couldn't. Jamie Sinclair was dead, killed by a stray bullet from Shad Clanton's gun, a bullet that tore through his cheekbone and out through the back of his skull.

CHAPTER IX

I count it a kindness that I cannot remember whole days that followed Jamie's death. I know that I was ill, out of my head for much of that fevered time. In my lucid moments, Clara or Father was always there. Dr. Dyer looked in mornings and evenings, and I can vaguely remember opening my eyes to see Sheriff Finn standing at the foot of my cot, looking down on me with an expression of sorrow and pity that so altered his appearance as to make me doubt that it really was my old hero standing there.

Mr. Grey looked in every day, but I do not remember seeing him. Father reported his visits to me. I can only suppose that, because I connected him with Jamie's death, my mind would let go its hold on reality whenever he came near. I did not want to see Josiah Grey.

People were kind. No one tormented me with questions. I learned later that Sheriff Finn let it be known that Jamie and I had warned him about Shad Clanton, and that in some confused way it was generally believed that Jamie and I were in the street on purpose to warn the Sheriff. They say the Reverend Owen David Owens made much of that at Jamie's burying.

There were some, a few, who found fault with Sheriff Finn. There are always those. As if a man facing a showdown with a professional killer has time to check the street for fools and children! The Sheriff never said anything to me about it. I doubt he said anything to those idiot carpers either. Explanations were not his style.

They say that Jamie's father began to die the day they laid the sod over Jamie. I saw him only once between then and the day of his own funeral. He had the look of a haunted man. All surplus flesh seemed to have dropped away, and his lightless eyes stared out from dark shadowed caverns, seeing nothing.

He came to the house, and Father brought him upstairs to see me. I tried to tell him how sorry I was, but he cut me off with a listless wave of the hand. "It was nobody's fault, boy," he said, his voice hollow and remote. "You are not to blame yourself."

"I am sure Charlie is grateful for your coming here," Father said, prompting me with his eyes.

"Thank you for coming," I said.

Again, there was that lifeless gesture, then he said, "I want you to have my boy's horse."

"Oh, Father, may I?" It was out before I could think, and when the shamelessness of it struck me, I wanted to sink through mattress, floor, cellar and the earth itself.

"Charlie, it is not wrong to want the horse," Father said.

"No, no, boy," said Mr. Sinclair in the same flat, dull voice. "There's no shame in it. Jamie would want ye to have it, and I cannot to bear to look at the bonny thing m'self. It is yours if your father does not object."

Father told me years later that he'd have let me have a team of horses, or just about anything else, if it would get me up out of that bed and back to being a boy again.

So I came to be master of Morgan le Fay. I have owned any number of horses since, but never a prettier nor a more willing creature than that little mare. Her temper was as sweet as Jamie's own had been, and I never rode her without feeling close, somehow, to that gentle smiling ghost who comes to me still in early waking dreams.

Mr. Sinclair went home to his great house and his silent, timorous wife. People came to call, to offer what comfort they could to this distant man who had never neighbored with them. But there was no solace for him. He had hired the gun that killed his boy, and the fatal bullet was now working in his own vitals. We buried him beside his son before the earth had fully healed over Jamie's windswept grave.

My own recovery, for all it was aided by the prospect of riding out on Morgan le Fay, was significantly slowed by my dread of returning to school. I just did not want to go back, but Father had strong notions about "soldiering," as he called it.

"Dr. Dyer says you are fit to go back, Charlie," he said, sitting on the bed beside me. "And I want you to go."

"Yes, Sir," I said, putting on the face of martyrdom.

"It matters, Charlie, or I would not press it. I know you have been through a bad time, but you cannot hide up here forever. The sooner you get on with your work, the sooner the pain will begin to ease." He reached out and smoothed my hair. "I am not saying you will forget Jamie. You never will. And you shouldn't. He was your friend. But grief can be selfish, Charlie. After a while, there is serious doubt as to whom we are grieving for.

"I want you up and out of this. You cannot do Jamie a bit of good by lying here, and you certainly are not doing yourself any good."

"Yes, Sir."

"I told Mr. Grey to expect you on Monday. He promises to help you catch up with your work, and that is what I want you to do." Father smiled. "Now come and have dinner with me. It has been too quiet for too long in this house. Clara needs bucking up. She has missed you at the table, and so have I."

It struck me then that Father could not know how hard it would be for me to go back to school, to have to show a hypocrite's smile for Mr. Grey, to see Sukey and pretend that nothing had changed, to look for Jamie and never find him there. But there was no help for it. I had to go.

On shaky legs, with dragging feet, I pulled myself up the path to the schoolhouse that cool gray morning,

fortified by Father's words and Clara's hotcakes. My one
hope was to be left alone, and I wrapped myself in the
dignity of sorrow as a means of achieving that end. It
worked pretty well.

A few scholars muttered hello; most kept their distance. Sukey, thank heaven, did not approach, but only
bestowed a look of pity as she whispered what I assumed
were cautionary words to the younger girls.

Mr. Grey did not make much of me. He said, "We
are all glad to have you back with us, Charlie. You may
take your place. You need not recite today."

Relieved, I slunk to my bench and slumped there
while the buzz of the schoolroom enveloped me. At
recess, I kept to myself, thinking it somehow out of
keeping with my new character to chatter and play. No
one bothered me; I suspect they had had their instructions, and I suppose they were no more comfortable
with my mournful presence than I'd have been with
their healthy cheerfulness.

I got through the afternoon session somehow, then
slipped out at the bell with a quickness inappropriate to
the character I had assumed.

"How did it go today?" Father asked over dinner
that night.

"Good," I said.

"How is Mr. Grey?"

"Good," I said.

"Well, I suppose you have work to do," said Father.
"Don't stay up too late, now."

"I won't," I said, and I escaped up the stairs.

Young as I was, I knew deep down that this could not continue. But, being young, I had to pretend that it would. Mr. Grey let me pretend for two days more. Then, after the noon recess of Thursday, before commencing the geography lesson, Mr. Grey said in an offhand way, "Oh, Charlie Prescott, would you be good enough to remain for a few minutes after dismissal?"

And I knew the game was up.

It was not a productive afternoon. My mind was all on the coming interview and, mercifully, Mr. Grey allowed my little drama a full run. He did not call on me. It was as if he recognized my rules and was willing to abide by them—for now. He went methodically about his business and, so far as I could observe, did not so much as glance in my direction until the session had run its course and the last scholar had left for home.

"Now, then, Charlie," he said, stepping down from the platform and coming up the splintered aisle to where I sat staring obstinately at the artwork carved in the surface of my bench, "we have to have a talk."

If he had waited for me to reply, he would have waited a long while. He sensed that, I suppose. At least he spared us both the awkwardness of silence. He took a seat across the aisle from me, crossed his long legs, clasped his hands over his knee, cocked his head, and fixed me with his good eye. "Charlie," he said, "I am going to speak plainly to you. I may not be able to say what I have to say in words that will go down easy. But I have thought long and hard about this, and I know that, rough or smooth, it has got to be said."

I dug my chin a bit deeper into my collarbone and braced myself.

"Charlie, you make me ashamed to be your friend." The words came with no particular force. He didn't raise his voice, nor did he lay any stress on any one word. He might as well have been reading off the ingredients on a patent medicine label. But the words stung. For all the smouldering anger I felt for him, they cut deep.

"I know Jamie was your friend, Charlie. We all know it. I respect your sorrow and the terrible shock that caused it. But I cannot and I do not respect the way you are using Jamie now."

"Using—?" I had to look up at that.

"Yes, Charlie, using." Mr. Grey uncrossed his legs, planted his feet on the floor and leaned forward. "Grief is sacred, Charlie. It is not a thing one carries like a flag. It is not a thing to be paraded. It is a thing one cherishes in his heart—or opens to those who have some claim to friendship."

My head sunk down again, even as the fire rose in my face.

"Look at me, Charlie." Josiah Grey's voice was sharp now, commanding. I raised my brimming eyes to his austere face. "You have been using Jamie Sinclair. I do not know why. I only know that it is so. And it is contemptible."

I think I could not have felt it more if he had struck me.

"You may think me harsh and unfeeling. But, Charlie, it is precisely because I do care—about you—

that I am speaking to you in this fashion. If I didn't care—" He shrugged, raising his hands and letting them fall limply into his lap. "Am I getting through to you at all?"

I think I nodded. I could not trust myself to speak.

"I hope so, Charlie. I purely hope so. Damn, boy, you are a scholar and a good one. For that alone I am out of all patience with this—this waste. But what is even more important is your character, the kind of boy you are, the man I hope you will become.

"I respected you, Charlie. I respected your loyalty, your grit, your style. Jamie was the better scholar, but of all my boys you were the one I expected to come shining through. You make mistakes, you can do some pretty foolish things sometimes, but I always figured that your mistakes were mistakes of the head, not of the heart. Your heart was always right, Charlie. That's what counted. That is all that counts ever. Can you believe that?"

I nodded, looking away to hide the tears.

"Then perhaps you can understand why I am so thoroughly disappointed in you." Mr. Grey reached out and took me by the shoulders, turning me towards him. "I wept for Jamie, Charlie. I still do. He was—golden. But he is gone. And you and I are here, and we have our work to do. The best way, the only way we have of honoring Jamie is to live our own lives as completely as we can, so maybe we can make up a little bit for the time he has lost."

I wanted so much just to bury my face in Mr. Grey's vest and sob. But I could not. I could only stare dumbly up at him through a wavering screen of tears.

"You were my first friend here, Charlie. You are just about my only friend now, and I believed that you thought of me as your friend. Well, I don't know what your definition of friendship is, but it seems to me that a friend is one who cares enough to bring his friend up short when he sees him going the wrong way. You are going the wrong way now, Charlie. And I would not be much of a friend if I did not try to head you off." He paused to let that sink in. Then he said. "And if you were my friend, you would care enough to tell me why you are going on like this."

Josiah Grey rose and stood looking down on me. "Might as well get it out, Charlie," he said. "We can't leave it here. Not like this. There has to be a reason for this—this performance of yours. I want to hear it. From you. Now."

"I know about you and Sukey Moncreiff."

He did not blink. He did not look away. He hooked his thumbs in the pockets of his vest and fixed me with his steady gaze. "Do you, Charlie?" he said. "Do you really know about Susannah and me?"

"Jamie and I were there that night, at the spring-house."

"Spying?"

"On Sukey. We saw her put a note in the hollow tree. We guessed that she was sweet on somebody. Some boy. We only meant to jump out and surprise her. We figured to scare her, and then run."

"But you didn't jump out."

I shook my head. "I heard you whistling, and I—I led Jamie off. I let on to be scared and I made a run for it."

"Why, Charlie?"

"I don't know. I wish I hadn't. Maybe if we'd have stayed there Jamie would not be dead."

"And maybe Sheriff Finn would be." Mr. Grey took a step or two nearer. "Tell me, Charlie, why did you lead Jamie away?"

I shrugged. "I didn't know what else to do. If he saw you with her—" I shrugged again.

"You were afraid Jamie would think ill of me? That he might talk? Make trouble, maybe?"

"I couldn't be sure, could I?"

Mr. Grey's hand came to rest on my shoulder. "No, you couldn't, Charlie. So you fooled one friend to save another."

"And one friend died." I couldn't help it. I knew I was rubbing Mr. Grey's face in it, but I couldn't let it go.

"Well, Charlie, if you are determined to put Jamie's death on me, I cannot prevent it. But I will not accept it. I will take any blame that is rightly mine, and I will carry it as best I can. But this was not my doing. I did not hire Shad Clanton; I did not set out to gun down Sheriff Finn; I did not fire the bullet that struck Jamie, and I did not send Jamie into the street to die."

"No!" I cried. "You didn't. I did!"

Mr. Grey put his arm around me and held me to him. "So that's the way of it?" he said. "Charlie,

Charlie, it was an accident, a stupid, one-in-a-million bad luck accident.

"Think, boy. That bullet could as easily have hit you. It was only chance that it did not." He patted me softly on the back. "I suppose Clara would say it was God's will. I don't know. I only know that you and Jamie were both there, and that Jamie was older—old enough, surely, and smart enough not to be led astray by you."

"But—but you know how Jamie was. He never argued with anybody."

"I wish he had, Charlie. Lord, how I wish he had. But that is not your fault. Can't you see that? The two of you were foolish, and one of you was unlucky. If you are looking for someone to blame, blame Clanton. Curse him, if it will make you feel better—although I must say that I think cursing is redundant in his case. Or you can blame Jamie's father, for whatever comfort that may bring you. I do not see how you can add anything to what he has already suffered. But don't blame yourself, Charlie. There is just no call to."

I mopped my eyes with my sleeve and sat up a little straighter.

"Feeling a little better?"

"Some," I said. "Thank you."

He rose. "Good. The thing is, Charlie, a man has got to be very careful when it comes to passing judgement. And when it comes to judging himself, well, it is a put-up job. There is no way he can get a fair trial in that court, and there is not a lawyer on earth who'd be fool enough to take his case.

"Let it go, Charlie. It is what Jamie would want."

"I'll try."

"And, Charlie?"

"Sir?"

"I appreciate your intentions in leading Jamie off that way, but don't spy on folks. It really is not worthy of you."

"I meant no harm, I—are you really sweet on her?" I had to ask it, I had to know.

"Would it disappoint you so very much?"

"But she—well, she's just a girl. You, you're a grownup man. And—and you're black."

"Born that way, Charlie," said Mr. Grey.

We eyed each other across a widening gulf of silence, and I could feel myself turning cold. It was not that I wanted to harden myself against Josiah Grey. Indeed, I hoped he would offer some plausible reason for his meeting with Susannah, make me believe that it was only to keep her quiet about his Pinkerton badge. But he gave me nothing. I wished that I were miles away, anywhere but in that gloomy schoolhouse alone with the man and his secrets.

"So, Charlie," he said, at last.

"You are sweet on her, then?"

He nodded, and I could feel bitter liquid rising in my throat, burning stuff that made me want to retch and be rid of it.

"I can't expect you to understand, Charlie," he said. "But I did hope that you would not judge me unfairly. And I hoped you would not think unkindly of Susannah. She is a fine young woman, and she is very dear to me."

There were several things I wanted to say about Sukey, but even in my hurt anger I had just sense enough to know that there was nothing I could say. I just wanted to get up and walk out of there. And I would have, too, but for a kind of morbid fascination in surveying the ruins of my friendship with Josiah Grey.

Here was a man I respected, a man who could stand up to Rufe Jakes or a room full of scholars with equal courage, a man of learning and grace who could stand level with my father and Sheriff Finn, and he was risking everything over a yellow-haired snip of a school-girl who would surely bring him to ruin.

And what could Sukey be thinking of? She surely knew that this little adventure of hers could come to no good. If word ever got out, if the men of Wind River Junction so much as suspected him, there was not a horse in the Territory swift enough to carry Mr. Grey beyond the reach of their outraged wrath.

"They will hang you," I said. "They will just haul you out to the edge of town some night and string you up like any horsethief."

"Who will?"

"People. Everybody. They won't stand for it." I looked up at him, so cool in his seeming unconcern, and I wanted to lash out, to sting him into awareness of just how dangerous a trail he was taking. "Do you think Old Moncreiff is going to sit still for his daughter's carrying on with a—a—"

"Say it, Charlie. Say it."

"Nigger." I bit down hard on the word.

"Does it bother you, Charlie? Does it make you want to see me hanged? Do you want me to die for daring to step over that invisible line?"

I hated him then for the way he kept stressing "you." But I said, "I don't want anybody to die."

"I call that right down friendly, Charlie. Thank you."

"Don't mock me."

"You are right, Charlie. I've no call to mock anyone." Mr. Grey turned and stepped up onto the platform. He sank wearily into his chair and sat for a long moment, staring at the floor. Then he raised his head and said, "It's not easy, is it, Charlie? Being my friend, I mean."

"No, Sir."

His smile was rueful. "I am not sure I could stand it myself. And yet I have valued your friendship, Charlie. I purely treasured it. But if I must let it go, I will. I do not want to bring you shame. If word got out—"

"I won't say anything," I muttered.

"Don't I know that, Charlie? Don't I know that you would never say anything? But this is more of a load than you are up to. I can't ask you to carry it. I would not want it on my conscience that your life here became unbearable because of your friendship for me."

"It isn't you," I protested. "It—it's you and Sukey. That's what is going to bring folks down on you, turn 'em against you, and—"

"And you, Charlie? Will it turn you against me? Or has it already?"

"I hate Sukey Moncreiff," I said.

"And I love her, Charlie," he said.

There was nothing more to say. Or if there was, I could not imagine what it might be.

"You have been a good friend to me, Charlie," said Mr. Grey, rising. "I had hoped that somehow you would be able to widen our friendship sufficiently to let Susannah in. But I see now that it was too much to ask. I thank you for your friendship. I hope that I can depend on you to take up your work again, because it matters. And I hope we can go on about our business here like men."

"I will do my work," I said.

"Fair enough. You had better go now. Clara will have supper waiting for you. I will see you in the morning, and kindly have those verbs memorized. I shall expect you to recite tomorrow."

I nodded. I couldn't speak. I knew that something had just died.

Walking out of that schoolhouse was the longest walk I'd ever taken. I paused at the door, turned and looked back. Mr. Grey, tall and imposing in the fading light, stood exactly as before, arms folded, head down, brooding in the long dark shadow that slanted across the raised desk, the platform, and the empty chair.

I think I heard him murmur a good night as I passed through the schoolhouse door.

Someday, maybe, I will be able to fathom why it is that when a body is down, when the world has turned into a great green apple, and it seems like nothing is ever going to be good again, it is precisely then that everyone else seems so disgustingly cheerful and bright. I do know that when I got home, Clara was humming away in her kitchen, rattling pots and pans in an orchestral accompaniment. I tried haunting the precincts with a melancholy face, but it gained me only a molasses cookie and a warning not to stray between then and dinner.

I tried it on Father when he came in, whistling and slapping his thigh with a rolled-up a copy of the *Clarion*, but he wasn't having any.

"I know it is hard trying to catch up on everything, Charlie," he said. "But don't look so glum. Why, if you were to work an extra hour every night, you would be caught up in no time."

"Yes, Sir."

"And if you could smile while you are about it, it would take even less time than that."

"Yes, Sir."

"As a matter of fact, tonight, instead of sitting up with Mr. Grey and me, you could go right up to your room and dig into those lessons just as soon as the table is cleared."

"I believe I will do that," I said. I had forgotten that this was Mr. Grey's regular evening to work with Clara. "Matter of fact, I could just as easy have a sandwich and a glass of milk up in my room. That way, I wouldn't lose time over dinner."

Father smiled. "Well, I don't believe you need to go on short rations," he said. "You can come to the table like any ordinary mortal, and then you can get cracking on your books."

I practically swallowed my dinner whole in my eagerness to clear out before Mr. Grey arrived. I made it. It cost me seconds on rhubarb pie, but I was upstairs and actually staring at a page of European history when I heard Clara welcome her tutor in. My concentration was sorely tested, but I dug my nails into my palms, gritted my teeth, and tried to ignore the muted sounds of talk and laughter from below. The close print made my eyes water and, to tell the truth, I was not consumed with interest in the forming of the Hanseatic League. In fact, my interest was so limited that I began to nod over my book, and finally I slept.

When I woke, my lamp was out. It was dark as the grave in my room, and about as quiet as graves generally are. But I could hear voices—and a different voice, a voice that made me sit bolt upright. I scuttled over to my listening place and, holding my breath, bent low and listened hard.

I heard my father say, "And so the shipment will go out on schedule?"

And that other voice replied, "We've no choice, Mr. Prescott. It has got to go."

Lord, my heart turned over twice. It was that voice, the voice I'd heard through a fog of sleep that night at old Daddy Jakes's soddy.

"I can muster a dozen men to ride escort," the voice continued, "and these are men who will do exactly as they are told."

"I have got me a dog like that," chimed in a third speaker, whom I knew immediately to be Sheriff Finn. "But he is still only just a dog."

"Then perhaps," returned that other voice, "perhaps we should pin a badge on your dog, Sheriff."

"Yes, Sir, if you want a dog instead of a man."

"What I want, what this community wants, is results, Sheriff. To date, they are uncommonly scarce."

"Gentlemen," said Father, "we are all agreed that these robberies have got to cease. Let us not fall out among ourselves now, or we shall accomplish nothing.

"Sheriff, do you see any objection to an armed escort?"

"No, Sir. I have no objections. I could point out that it has been tried before now. And I could point out that it has failed. But objections? No. It ain't my gold, and they ain't my men, and I doubt I have any kinfolk among 'em. If they are of a mind to die, it is not my place to try and prevent 'em."

"What makes you so certain they will die?" asked the third man.

"Look at the hist'ry of the thing. Ever' blessit time there has been a shipment, the word has got out and people have got permanently inconvenienced."

While the third man was making up his argument, I made up my mind. I pulled on my boots, opened the window, and slid out into the cool darkness. I stepped off into the arms of my accommodating tree and clambered down. Keeping low and close to the shadowing walls of the house, I slipped around to the front and, on tiptoe, peered in at the parlor window.

Father was standing near the stove in his best Daniel Webster attitude. The Sheriff, his back to me, was slouched in the spindle-backed chair that Grandma

Prescott had brought with her when she and Grandpa had come out to Nebraska from Ohio. And in the horse-hair armchair, his high-domed massive head resting against the antimacassar, sat Mr. Jock Moncreiff.

My heels came down. I turned and sat right down on the ground, my back against the clapboards, and tried to collect my thoughts.

It was Moncreiff's voice I had heard that night at the Jakes's place. That was certain. But what on earth would our banker and foremost citizen have to do with that trash? He could barely bring himself to respond to a polite "good morning" from the ordinary run of mortals, and yet he'd had dealings with Rufe Jakes—dealings that included bringing a bottle with him when he came to call. And it must have been Moncreiff who delivered that ransom note. Who else could it have been? I shook my head hard, trying to get my brains going. I just could not picture that buttoned-up starchy old citizen heaving a rock through our front window. And yet, and yet—

The front door opened, and I went flat. I heard some pretty brisk "good nights" and saw the banker, his face like a clenched fist under his tall hat, step out of the light and march down our brick walk, austere and dignified as becomes a man whose life is spent in the getting and begetting of money. He climbed stiffly into his rig, touched up his horse and went spinning off into the night. Moments later, Sheriff Finn made his exit. I followed him.

I gave him a good lead, then set out, meaning to catch up with him at his office where we could talk freely. As usual with him, the Sheriff didn't hurry. He sauntered along, pausing here and there to look in at an alleyway or a window, just making sure the town was lashed up for the night. I did my best to keep some distance between us, but at the rate he was moving, I'd have done better to go the other way and maybe pass through China and come up with him on my way back.

He came to a halt in front of Briscoe's place, bit the end off a cigar, spat and fired up. I ducked into an alley, determined to wait till the thunk of his bootheels told me it was time to commence trailing again. It seemed to me I'd waited about a week when I gave it up, figuring that the Sheriff had taken root right through the sidewalk. Following him was only a game anyway. I knew he would not send me home without a hearing. But I was enjoying myself, and it disappointed me to abandon my play. Still, it wouldn't do to stay out all night. There was always the risk that Father might look in on me on his way to bed. So I stepped out of hiding and saw to my confusion that the Sheriff had moved on. The street was as deserted as one of those plague cities of the Middle Ages that Mr. Grey had told us about at school.

Feeling a bit foolish, and not at all pleased with myself, I began to trot for the jailhouse. As I passed the littered alley between the Chinese laundry and the Good Time Cafe, I lost about six years' growth. A hand shot out of the shadows, seized me by the shoulder, and snaked me clean off my feet and into the alley.

"Out kinda late, ain't you, Charlie?" said the Sheriff, letting go his grip and grinning down at me like a fox eyeing a prize pullet that has wandered too far from the henhouse.

"Lord A'mighty," I said, "you about scared the tripe out of me."

"Well, tighten up, boy, and speak your piece. What was you trackin' me for?"

"You spotted me?"

"Charlie, I would not be here now if I had not growed eyes in the back o' my head. Shoot, I heard you before we was well clear o' your pa's gate, and I made sure it was you when you thought I was lookin' in at Hoxie's hotel. You make a pretty poor tracker, Charlie. You might do for a Pinkerton, but if you have got any notions of takin' up this line o' work, you have better give up that school and go live with the Arapaho. You're young yet, and they could maybe learn you somethin' if you was to apply yourself.

"What was it you wanted to see me about?"

"Sheriff, you remember that time I was being held prisoner by Rufe Jakes, and I told you that someone had come out there during the night? Someone I thought I knew but couldn't place?"

"Well, I can remember when you was took prisoner right enough, Charlie. But blamed if I can recall your sayin' anything about any visitors. You certain you told me?"

Then I remembered that it was Mr. Grey I'd told, and it was clear that he had not troubled himself to pass on the information to the Sheriff. It was an awkward place, but it was no time to shilly-shally. "I told Mr. Grey," I said. "I forgot you weren't there when I told him."

"Oh."

"Thing is, someone was there that night. And it must have been that someone who flung that note through the window. I—I was so sleepy that I couldn't come awake enough to get a look at him, but I heard his voice. And I knew it, but I couldn't place it. It's been haunting me since till it's come near to driving me crazy."

"Yes, I have known that to happen."

"Well, now I know who it was. Only I can't believe it, because it doesn't make any sense."

"Well, suppose you just try 'er out on me. Who was it?"

"Mr. Moncreiff."

"Mon—! Charlie, are you sure?" Sheriff Finn seized my arms and brought his face down level with mine.

"It was, Sheriff. I couldn't be mistaken. I know it sounds crazy, but he was there that night. I'd swear to it on a stack of Bibles."

"Boy, we have got to make medicine."

"What are you going to do?"

"By rights, we ought to go and lay this thing before your pa. And I suppose the decent thing would be to bring in that Pinkerton, although I—well, let that alone. Come on, Charlie, we are going back to your house. I reckon your pa won't lick you for slippin' out o' camp when he hears what we got to tell him."

Father came to the door in his shirtsleeves, his braces down, his collar undone. If he was not pleased at being disturbed so late, he was even less pleased to see me standing there.

"What's this, Sheriff?" he said, running me through with a piercing glance. "No trouble, I hope."

"Well, yessir, Mr. Prescott. Some. But not on the boy's account. He's done us a good turn, looks like, and I thought we had better have a talk about it."

Father sniffed. "I am sure it must be important for you both to come calling so late."

His sarcasm was not lost on me, but I counted on the Sheriff's report to take some of the heat off, and I was not disappointed.

"Jock Moncreiff," my father said, purely amazed. "Why, Sheriff, I could not be more astonished if you told me it was the Reverend Owen David Owens."

"Kinda took me that way, too, Mr. Prescott."

"But what on earth could Jock Moncreiff have in common with Rufe Jakes?"

"I been askin' myself that all the way over here," replied the Sheriff, as Father waved him to a chair. "And the way I figger it, he meant to recruit old Rufe into that little private army o' his that is supposed to ride out with the next shipment."

"Hum. That would be setting a thief to catch a thief, certainly," said Father, stroking his clean-shaven chin.

"Well, now, I ain't all that certain that Mr. Moncreiff meant to catch a thief."

"Then what—?"

"I think Mr. Moncreiff is a thief."

Father was about to object, but the Sheriff held up a forestalling hand. "Look at 'er this way, Mr. Prescott. Every time we have set a trap, the rats has run off with the cheese. We knowed blamed well there was a leak. I had my money on another hoss, I admit. Well, I was wrong."

"You mean Sinclair?"

Sheriff Finn nodded. "Meanin' no disrespect to the dead, Sinclair was my choice. I couldn't see the Doctor in it, and Major Hoxie—well, meanin' no disrespect to the livin' either, I judged he hadn't brains enough nor sand enough for a job that size. And you weren't ever in the runnin'."

"Thank you," murmured Father, a suspicious twinkle in his eye.

"You are welcome," said the Sheriff gravely. "So that left Sinclair and Moncreiff. Now our banker is a mighty man, a man of standing and repute. It just couldn't enter into my thinkin' that a old nabob like that could turn his hand to anything downright crooked.

"Oh, he ain't above foreclosin' on a widder or puttin' the squeeze on some pore nester that has run through his luck. And I don't doubt but what he has bought a judge or two, or maybe played a fifth ace in the kinds o' games them fellers play with railroaders and congressmen. But that's all by the way and of no account in my business. You got to expect that from bankers. It's in the breed."

Father laughed out loud, and I sat a little easier in the spindle-back chair.

"Besides," the Sheriff went on, "to a man on my wages, it just don't seem possible that a man like Moncreiff could want more'n he has already got, which is foolish, o' course, because with them kind there ain't no such a thing as enough."

"And yet," said Father, "as I recall, it was when Mr. Sinclair hired Shad Clanton that you ruled him out of the running."

"True enough."

"Then why, when Charlie tells us that there was business between Moncreiff and Rufe Jakes—?"

"Ah, well, you got to remember that it ain't Moncreiff's gold," broke in the Sheriff, a shrewd expression on his freckled, goodhumored face. "Y'see, Sinclair was lookin' after his own. But Moncreiff now, he deals in other folks' money. Why, if we was to get a look at his papers, I bet we would find that Moncreiff ain't out a penny by any of these here holdups. More'n that, I will wager a bottle of Cassidy's best bonded sippin' whiskey that we'd find he holds notes or liens or some such kind of paper on them mines that's been shippin' the gold through here. Why, if them mine owners was to go bust, it would make your head spin to see how quick old Moncreiff would scoop 'em up. He would be in the minin' business to stay, and there wouldn't be no more holdups neither, not if he had to hire the entire Mexican army to ride herd on every shipment he sent."

It was plain to see that Father was impressed by the Sheriff's argument. He sat silent for a long moment, then shook his head and said, "Well, it is an interesting theory, Sheriff. Mighty interesting. But it is only a theory."

"Come again?"

"No proof," Father said. "You can't just ride out to Moncreiff's place and arrest him without some hard evidence that will convince a jury that our leading citizen is a common thief."

Sheriff Finn scratched his head. "Well, now, your idea of what is common is a leetle different from mine, Mr. Prescott. But even I know that we have got to get the goods on him. I been sittin' here sortin' out a couple-three ways we might skin the skunk, and it appears to me that our best line is—"

We never did get to learn what the Sheriff's notion was, for he was interrupted by a sudden and thunderous banging on our front door. I nearly jumped out of my socks, and the Sheriff, leaping to his feet, cried, "Jee-rusalem! Somebody is tryin' to bust your door down."

Father, gone suddenly paler than ordinary, strode to the door and yanked it open to find Sukey Moncreiff standing there, barefoot, wild-eyed, her hair in disarray.

"Susannah," my father began, but she spied the Sheriff and rushed past Father and all but flung herself on the Sheriff.

"Sheriff! Oh, Sheriff," she cried, "you have got to stop them. They mean to murder Mr. Grey!"

"Hey, now, Sis," said the Sheriff, patting her shoulder awkwardly with a huge freckled paw, "simmer down. We will help ya all we can, but you must calm yourself and talk plain or we c'n be of no use to ya."

He led her to the sofa and sat her down. She did look a sight. She had only a shawl thrown over her thin flannel nightdress; her feet were cut and bruised in a score of places, and as she raised her blanched, dis-traught face to the Sheriff, the lamplight revealed a thin scarlet trickle running down from the corner of her mouth.

Father roused me from my gaping. "Go fetch Clara, Charlie. Tell her to bring linen, the salve, and a basin of warm water."

I ran to do as I was bid, then hurried back so as not to miss anything.

"—and my father has gone to get some men," Susannah was saying. "He locked me in my room, but I got out and—and I ran—ran—" and Sukey Moncreiff broke down and wept.

Father bent over her, his eyes sad and kind. "Susannah," he said, "did you warn Mr. Grey?"

She shook her head. "I—I just couldn't run anymore. I saw your light, and I—"

"Hush, now," Father said. "Hush. Here's Clara. Clara, this poor child is done in. Would you please see to her hurts, then put her to bed in the spare chamber? I would take it kindly if you would sit with her a while."

"Oh, you poor lamb," murmured Clara, as she knelt to bathe Susannah's feet. "You just let Clara take care of you now."

I couldn't understand why I felt like crying just then. Perhaps it was the tenderness in Clara's voice. Perhaps it was because, for the first time since I'd known her, I could feel something like compassion for Sukey. Whatever it was, I know that even now I cannot recall Clara's beautiful hands tending those lacerated milky feet without an unaccountable smarting of the eyes.

"Mr. Prescott," said Sheriff Finn, "I think I had better get on out to the schoolhouse. Time's short."

Father went to the old hair trunk by the coat rack and fetched out the gunbelt he had worn in the war. "I will ride with you, Sheriff," he said.

Sheriff Finn seemed to hesitate. Then he said, "Can you shoot that thing?"

Father almost smiled. "I remember which end the bullet comes out at," he said. "What we want is numbers, Sheriff. If we can muster enough guns, there may not be any shooting."

The Sheriff's face looked strangely old. "If we mean to save that Pinkerton, we haven't time to round up help. I ain't altogether sure we'd find many willing to help. Truth is, I ain't right down proud to take a hand myself."

Father and Sheriff Finn appeared to be reading each other's eyes, then Father said, "So be it, then. If we can make the schoolhouse ahead of Moncreiff's men, we may be able to get Mr. Grey into hiding and avoid the whole unpleasantness."

"Seems to me the time to avoid it was about an hour before that fool Pinkerton decided to go a-courtin' out to Moncreiff's place," growled the Sheriff. He tugged his hat low on his brow and said, "Let's go, then."

As they made the door, Father turned and, looking directly at me with a look that brooked no argument, said, "Charles, you make yourself useful to Clara, then go directly to bed. I will expect to find you there when I return."

"Yes, Sir," I said, meek as mice.

But I had my fingers crossed behind my back.

CHAPTER X

Clara kept me on the jump for about another quarter of an hour after Father and the Sheriff had left. I had to fetch and carry, turn down the bed, brew some tea, and just generally step to Clara's tune. But I kept my ears open, and I was able to piece together enough of a story to ease my itch to know.

Sukey, it seems, had counted on her father's absence and arranged to meet Mr. Grey in the spring-house as before. Unfortunately for them, old Moncreiff got home a bit early—early enough to spy a man leaving the premises. There were some hard words spoken and some blows struck before Moncreiff was able to wring from Sukey the identity of her caller. He then locked her in her room and rode off to round up his men.

I had to give Sukey credit for more sand than I'd have looked for in any girl I'd ever met. She didn't sit around vaporing and wringing her hands. As soon as her father had cleared out, she smashed through a panel of her door with a chair leg, and came running on purpose to save Josiah Grey. She had worn herself out in the effort, and taken a considerable risk in the bargain. It was enough almost to change my thinking where Susannah was concerned. I made up my mind to think it all over when I found time, but time was not something I had a whole lot of that evening.

So soon as Clara released me from duty, I made a show of going upstairs to my bed. But my mind was already made up. If Susannah Moncreiff had the grit to risk what would surely be coming to her when her father learned of her escape, then I reckoned I ought to be able to stand whatever punishment Father handed me for disobeying him. Besides, there was Mr. Grey to think of.

I was not over my mad with him, but there was one fact that came through strong and clear. Josiah Grey may have been a fool about Susannah, but he had been a friend to me. And any differences I might have had with him were swallowed up in fear, fear for his life.

He had taught me so much—and not just Latin, either, or how to box. He had taught me about friendship. And it was plain to me that a friend would not let a little thing like a whipping stand between him and his friend. Besides, hadn't Father said they would need all the guns they could muster?

It wasn't much, but I did have a little light fowling piece that could scatter shot with a respectable bang. And there was my little brass pistol that I was absolutely forbidden to use except under supervision on July 4th and Election Night. I don't know that it could have done any serious damage, but it did shoot.

I lowered my hardware to the ground with a length of fishline, then took my usual route down the branches of the box elder. It would have suited me to fetch Morgan le Fay, but she was stabled at the livery. I could not take the risk of running into Father, and I could not think how to get around old John Chapman, the stableman. No, my best bet was to leg it crosslots and hope to goodness that I ran into nobody. So I shoved my pistol in my waistband, caught up my bird gun, and made tracks.

There was no moon, and there was the smell of rain on the wind as I made my way up the rise to the border of the roadway. It struck me then that it was as well I was on foot. The little mare could easily have missed her footing in the dark and done herself serious harm. Besides, it was certain that sound of her iron-shod feet would have announced my arrival sooner than might be convenient.

I halted about a quarter of a mile from the schoolhouse and shucked my boots. I was keeping to the edge of the gravel, but there was no sense in taking the least chance. I fished a shell from my pocket and loaded the bird gun, then stole up the rise on stockinged feet.

I had not gone far when I heard the approach of horses. I sidestepped into the brush and scrunched down to wait. In about two shakes, along came two men riding abreast. They halted just a bit up the road from where I was hid.

"Hear anything?" Father said, his voice low but carrying in the wind.

"No. And I don't know whether to be glad or sorry," said the Sheriff. "It could mean that—"

A shot rang out, putting a period to the Sheriff's speculations. "Let's go," he said, and spurts of sand and gravel rattled on the young leaves as the horses dug for the schoolhouse. I lit out after them, not troubling now about silence and caution. They could not have heard me over the hoofbeats anyway.

As I drew up puffing and blowing at the edge of the schoolyard, a regular fusillade broke out, and I came perilously near to disgracing myself. But I tightened up and took in the situation.

Riders, there must have been ten or a dozen of them, were loping around and around the schoolhouse like a living carousel. They carried torches, most of them, and the ripe stink of coal oil scented the air as the flames leaped and danced in the breeze.

Strange, even now I can recall the sinister beauty of the spectacle—horses flowing in and out of the shadows, the rhythmic drumming of hoofs, the eerie play of the torchlight, the creak and clink of leather and steel, the flashes of flame and the sharp crack of the guns. It was the Devil's own charivari, and there was no doubt in my mind that Satan himself was riding the Wind River Range that night.

How he did it is still a wonder to me, but Sheriff Finn rode smack into that ring and brought up a bellow from down around the region of his spleen. The shooting came to a ragged stop, and the carousel ground to a skittering halt. The riders bunched up, their torches casting a circle of wavering light around them. Jock Moncreiff, hatless, sparse strands of iron-gray hair blowing free, urged his mount forward a few paces. In the flickering light, his harsh features took on the aspect of an avenging phantom-come-lately from the confines of the Pit.

"You've got no business here, Sheriff," the old man cried. "Go back to town now, and you won't get hurt."

"I appreciate your concern for my health, Moncreiff," drawled Sheriff Finn, "but I mean to stay."

Moncreiff glared undiluted hate. Then he turned on Father. "You, Prescott, talk sense to him."

"I can't," Father said. "I am only a deputy."

"You see how it is, Moncreiff," said the Sheriff. "We are here to keep the peace, which is my job, and I am a man that takes pride in earning his wages."

"We haven't broken any law."

"Not yet, maybe. Although you are endangering public property with them torches, and I reckon I can find one or two other statutes to cite when I get back to my quarters."

"And you call yourself a white man."

"Well, a man, at any rate. I don't need no mob to do my fightin' for me."

"That nigger has tampered with my daughter!" Moncreiff roared. "And I mean to see he gets what's coming to him."

"Well, Sir, I am not sure what you mean by 'tampered,' but if the schoolmaster has broke a law, I will arrest him and hold him for trial."

"Aw, to hell with this palaver," came a voice from the ranks of Moncreiff's men. "Let's just torch the schoolhouse and roust the nigger out."

Sheriff Finn unshucked his gun. "That mouth sounds like it belongs to a white-livered coyote that wears the name of Jackson. And if I was you, Thad, I would put a button on it. Incitin' to riot could get you a ticket to the territorial prison."

"Shut your head, Thad," growled Moncreiff, swinging around in the saddle. Then he turned back to the Sheriff. "Be sensible, Finn. There doesn't have to be a riot. We mean to take that nigger and teach him a lesson. There is not a white man in the territory who would vote to convict us if we did kill him, and you know it."

"I would," Father said.

"Yes, you would, wouldn't you, Prescott?" Moncreiff barked a sardonic laugh. "I have had doubts about you all along, and your being here tonight confirms them."

"Odd," said Father, "I was about to say those identical words to you."

"Mr. Prescott, I believe that my bank holds a note on your press. I should remind you that I can buy and sell you twice over."

"Well, you could buy the press," Father said.

"Look here, Moncreiff," the Sheriff broke in. "It is late, and I am missing any amount of shut-eye. So why don't you fellers just get along home and leave this business to me. I will investigate your complaint—"

"No, thank you, Sheriff. The teacher needs a lesson, and I mean to give it to him."

"What kind o' lesson, exactly?"

Moncreiff replied in terms too coarse to bear repeating. But the meaning was mutilation. And he flourished an ugly little gelding knife by way of demonstrating his seriousness of purpose.

"Can't let you do it, Moncreiff," said the Sheriff.

"You are not very bright, Sheriff, but I thought you knew how to count. There are only two of you."

Sheriff Finn laughed. "I may not be bright, as you say, but you can't believe I would be so blamed foolish as to ride out here without help. Me and Mr. Prescott rode in to parley. I got deputies back there in the brush that are just waitin' on my signal to ride in here and tidy up the place."

"Bluff, Finn, sheer bluff," crowed Moncreiff. He rose in his stirrups and called out, "If there is anyone back there, sing out!"

Sometimes I marvel at my capacity to amaze myself. I guess I amazed some others, too, not excepting Father and Sheriff Finn. I shut my eyes tight, pointed my shotgun at the stars, and pulled the trigger.

There were no flies on Sheriff Finn. Before the echo had died away, he bellowed, "God damn it, Homer, the man said to sing out, not shoot. You might a-killed somebody."

I would have given a twenty-dollar gold piece, if I'd had one, to have a glimpse of Father's face. But he and the Sheriff had their backs to me. A remarkable uneasiness broke out among Moncreiff's riders, though, and I can't say that I blame them. It could not have been a comfortable feeling to know that there was a gun out there in the darkness, in unpredictable hands.

"Well, Moncreiff, 'pears like you have got to fish or cut bait," declared the Sheriff.

"You bring in your deputies, Sheriff, and we will discuss it."

My heart collided with my liver. Why, if I were to walk out into that circle of flickering light, those that didn't die laughing would drop dead from shock. And if there were any survivors, they would surely finish what they had set out to do, even if it meant killing Father and Sheriff Finn. I rammed another shell into my bird gun and commenced to circling toward the rear of the schoolhouse. It occurred to me that if I was to fire off another round from another location, it might persuade Moncreiff that the Sheriff did indeed have hands sufficient to back his play.

"There ain't nothing to discuss," the Sheriff said. "I have a badge here that says I am the law. And the law says there is to be no killin' nor no maimin'. You fellers just ride out peaceable, and that'll be the end of it."

I was directly back of the schoolhouse now, and having no idea in the world of what to do, I began moving slowly toward it.

"I won't throw in my hand over one more gun, Sheriff, not while I have got ten to back me. I don't believe your bushwhacking deputy wants to see you shot." Moncreiff raised his voice, but he needn't have troubled. I could hear him fine where I was. "So he had better show himself. And that goes for anybody else that might be hiding out there."

I fired off my pistol.

"Take it easy, Fred!" cried the Sheriff. "We are still parleying here!"

I wished I dared answer, but I had sense enough to know that my voice wasn't up to it. It hadn't changed yet, and there was just no way I could produce a grown-up masculine growl.

"Well, that's two," allowed Moncreiff. "But you will need an army if you mean to stop us, Sheriff."

"I make it three!" called a voice from somewhere in the region of the clouds, and I heard a solid click like a bolt going home.

"The nigger's in the belfry!" someone yelled.

"Pick him off!" roared Moncreiff. "Pick him off or he will kill us all!"

Horses squealed and cavorted like mad as the bullets whined like angry bees. More than a few dinged into the bell, but I did not stand around to enjoy the music. Hugging the shadows, I slithered along the schoolhouse wall till I came to a window. Under cover of all that racket, it was no trouble to break in, and I didn't stand on ceremony, but just shattered the pane, and reached in and slipped the latch.

I dropped my weapons in, then hoisted myself up over the sill. I was hanging half in and half out of the lightless schoolroom when I felt a cold hard pressure against my temple, just about my left eye.

"Don't shoot, for pity's sake!" I cried.

"Charlie!" Strong hands drew me in and stood me up in the close darkness. "What are you doing here, you little fool? Do you mean to get yourself killed?"

"N-no, Sir. I came to help."

Josiah Grey let out a gust of air from deep in his lungs. "Does your father know you are here?"

"No, Sir."

"Well, Charlie, we are in a tight place and no mistake. I couldn't risk shooting for fear of hitting your father or the Sheriff. And now there is no telling what will happen with you in here. I can't just stand here till they storm the place for fear they will make buzzard's meat of you. And I can't—"

"Give it up, nigger!" came a bellow from the schoolyard. "You are outnumbered, and there is no way you can make a run for it."

"Sounds like they have got the drop on Sheriff Finn," muttered Mr. Grey. "I do wish there was a back door on this schoolhouse. If I live to meet the architect, I will have something to say to him."

"Couldn't you go out the window?"

"And how far would I get? You don't happen to have a horse tied up out there, I suppose?"

"No, Sir. I came on foot."

There came another shout from the schoolyard. "We will give you three minutes, nigger. Then we are going to burn you out!"

"What are you going to do, Mr. Grey?" I was so scared that I could hardly get the words out through the chattering of my teeth.

"I don't know, Charlie. I'm about prayed out. I—Charlie, would you take it unkindly if I were to use you as a hostage?"

"Will it help?"

"It might. It is a lot better than being burned alive, that's certain. The main thing is, it can keep you from getting yourself killed. I have got to let them know you are in here. If I can convince them that I mean to use you as a shield, I might just be able to put some distance between them and me. Are you game?"

Whatever anger I had been saving drained away. "I'm game," I said.

"All right. Now you have got to act scared, Charlie. And I mean scared to death."

I could have told him that I would not need to do much acting, but I guessed he knew that.

"When I make my play, I will be holding you in front of me. They are mad, but they are not crazy. They won't dare to shoot for fear of hitting you. All you have got to do is convince them that you are being forced to go with me, that you believe I will let you die to save myself. Can you do it?"

"I will do my best."

"Good." Josiah Grey whipped out a huge white handkerchief and knotted a corner of it to the barrel of his rifle. He sidled up to a front window, eased it open, and stuck the improvised flag through.

"You giving it up, nigger?" called Moncreiff.

"I want to parley," replied Mr. Grey.

"We have nothing to parley about. Just come out and take what's coming to you, or die in the schoolhouse. There is no other choice."

"I think there is. I have a bargain to offer, one you can't afford to pass up."

"What bargain?"

"I have the Prescott boy in here with me."

"Charlie!" There was no mistaking Father's voice.

"I—I'm here, Father," I croaked.

"You all right, boy?" called Moncreiff.

"Y-yes, Sir. B-but I'm awful scared. Please don't shoot. I don't want to die!"

It got very quiet in the schoolyard. Then I could hear a muted flurry of talk, punctuated by some pretty ripe language.

Then Moncreiff sang out. "You wouldn't hide behind a kid, Schoolteacher. You haven't got the will to see him hurt."

"The hell I haven't," cried Mr. Grey, and he pinched me hard on the arm, forcing a yip out of me that made even him jump.

"He's got a knife!" I yelled, inspired.

"Charlie, you are a caution," murmured Josiah Grey. "We will make a Pinkerton of you yet."

"Mr. Grey," Father shouted, "don't hurt my boy!"

"Then make your friends give this up. I mean it, Mr. Prescott. I bear you no ill will, but I do not intend to die tonight. Give me a good horse and a fair start, and I will leave the boy at the edge of town. Unharmed. That is my best offer. You can take it or leave it."

"You really going to take me with you?" I whispered.

"I wish I could, Charlie, and that's a fact. But, no, I mean to leave you here, only they mustn't know that. I must say, your father has got some acting talent, too. Must run in the family."

We could hear Father pleading my cause with Jock Moncreiff, and I was in a terrible sweat, as much as I'd have been had I feared any harm from Josiah Grey.

"I can't let that nigger go," Moncreiff was saying. "He has disgraced my daughter and insulted me. I could never face my neighbors again if that black bastard was to get away with this."

"Can you face yourself as a murderer?" Father said.

"Which is what you will be if the boy dies," declared Sheriff Finn, "and I will be obliged to see you hang for it."

"And my men will stand by and see you do it, I suppose." Moncreiff snorted like a blown horse. "You are sadly short on sense, Finn. I wonder you can find your face with your fork."

"I can find a polecat in the dark, Moncreiff, and in my line o' work that is sufficient."

"You will be looking for work when this night is over, I can tell you that."

"That's as may be," allowed the Sheriff. "But right now, as sheriff, I am ordering you and your men to clear out and let Mr. Prescott's boy have his chance."

"Damn it, Finn, I don't want the boy hurt any more than you do. But I mean to have a crack at that nigger. He won't hurt that youngun, and you—"

Mr. Grey dug a sharp poke into my short ribs and I let out another yell. "Father, save me!" I bawled.

Mr. Grey started to laugh. And that got me to laughing, too. We couldn't help it. I can't say even now if I was having hysterics, or if it was just one of those silly fits that will take a body in the most inappropriate times and places. It was a strange sight, I am sure, if there had been anyone to see it. There we were, trapped in that schoolhouse, and giggling like a pair of prize idiots.

"Bite your lip, Charlie," gasped Mr. Grey. "If they hear us laughing, we are lost for sure."

"Let the boy show himself at the window, nigger," roared Moncreiff.

Mr. Grey eased me over. "Let them see you," he said, "but for God's sake look scared now."

I tried. I am not sure they could see my expression anyway, but I could make them out pretty well in the torchlight. Father and the Sheriff were standing next to Mr. Moncreiff. The vigilantes, if you can call them that, were bunched up to one side.

"Are you all right, Charlie?" Father called.

"Yes, Sir, only awful scared. I want to go home."

Sheriff Finn detached himself from the group and took a stand directly in front of the schoolhouse. "Moncreiff," he said "you have to let them pass."

"You haven't got sufficient guns to be giving orders, Finn."

"No, Sir, but you will be dead before your bully boys can do for me."

I heard the ominous click of the hammer of the Sheriff's revolver.

"Finn, I will have your badge in my pocket come morning."

The Sheriff did not reply directly. He said, "Mr. Prescott, you will please to stand aside. The light is uncertain, and I would feel just terrible if I was to wing you by mistake. There now. Thank you."

"Jackson, you bring up my horse, and don't be long about it. I am gettin' a mite nervous, and my patience is about to run out."

Thad Jackson, he of the loud mouth, stepped around lively and secured the Sheriff's mount.

"Lead him up here nice and easy, then get back to that pack you run with," the Sheriff commanded. He took hold of the bridle and led his horse up to the step.

"Now then, I am going to summon the schoolteacher. He is goin' to be holdin' the boy, I expect, so I will take it unkindly if any fool was to try his luck in this light. I am partial to that boy, and I guess I would just nacherly have to kill the man who was to harm him in any way.

"Back off, Moncreiff. Let's have room, here. We will need it."

Slowly, reluctantly, Moncreiff backed away, gun in hand and hate in his contorted face.

"All right now, Schoolteacher," called the Sheriff, his voice just as calm and natural as if he were passing the time of day with the loafers in front of Briscoe's store, "you have the face cards. Here's my horse and there's the road. Make your play."

Mr. Grey seized me around the waist. "This is it, Charlie. I believe you will come to no harm. Just make it look good and convincing."

"Yes, Sir."

"And, Charlie—"

"Sir?"

"Thank you."

Mr. Grey caught me up in front of him and came through the door, his left arm circling my middle, his right hand couching his Sharps rifle. I flailed my arms and legs around lively and tried to look wild. I think I did it pretty well. At any rate, the men fell back as Mr. Grey boosted me into the saddle and climbed up behind me. He drummed his heels on the horse's ribs, and we went flying out of the schoolyard.

It was a good plan, I guess, but Mr. Grey's back was just too tempting a target. A shot split the air, then another. Mr. Grey pitched sideways out of the saddle, and I was obliged to grab a fistful of mane to keep from going right over. By the time I was able to bring the animal to a halt and turn his head, the shooting was general, and I was a far piece down the road.

Sobs rose in my throat. Mr. Grey was surely gone, and Father might be lying dead in the schoolyard. With no caution or thought, I kicked up the Sheriff's horse and flew back at a gallop. The guns were silent as I pulled up before the schoolhouse door.

Father was there, on his feet and apparently unhurt, his face deathly white in the last light of a torch that someone had dropped in the skirmish.

"Father!" I cried, sliding down from the saddle.

"Charlie! Thank God! Where is Mr. Grey?"

"I—I don't know. He—he went down. I didn't see him again. Are they all gone?"

"All that were left, yes." Father shook his head as if to clear his brain. "Moncreiff is dead. Sheriff Finn shot him when he shot Mr. Grey. The rest of the gang hadn't much stomach for a fight after that. They—somebody, I don't know who it was—rode into me and bowled me over. I was unconscious for a minute or two, I think. I remember seeing the Sheriff—oh, Lord, Charlie, the Sheriff! Give me that torch!"

I passed the flickering light to him, and Father began to survey the yard, sweeping his light in wide arcs. I stayed close, feeling that I would never willingly leave his side again.

And we found Sheriff Finn. He was lying face down in the worn place near the pump, a dark stain showing sinister and wide on the back of his rumpled coat.

"Hold the light, Charlie," Father said, his voice tight and strained.

Tears streamed down my face as Father knelt and gently turned the Sheriff face up. I wanted to scream out in protest, to call my old hero back from the border of that shadowy range, but I knew I must not.

The Sheriff's eyelids flickered, then opened wide. "Hey, Mr. Prescott," he said, his voice pitifully weak. "Hey, Charlie. You—you all right?"

"I—I'm fine, Sheriff. Finer than frog hair."

He grinned, then grimaced as the lead worked in his bones. "I think I messed it up pretty good," he said.

"No, Huck," said Father. "You did fine, really fine."

A blissful smile broke out on the bloodless face and the Sheriff struggled to raise himself. With his weight on his right elbow, he lifted his left arm and pointed. Father and I turned to see the ashen face of Josiah Grey.

"It's old Jim!" said the Sheriff, his voice suddenly strong. "Hey, Jim!"

And he fell back and died.

I think my childhood died there in the schoolyard with Sheriff Finn. It was there that I had my last real cry. Father let me sob it out in the shelter of his arms. Then he said, "Charlie, we have lost one friend tonight. If we tarry here, we stand to lose another. We have got to get Mr. Grey to safety. It is what the Sheriff wanted. God knows he paid dearly for it."

"And I can never believe it was worth it," said Josiah Grey, his voice hard, changed, different from the voice I knew.

"Never is a long time," Father said. "And time is not something we have a whole lot of. How badly are you hurt?"

Mr. Grey shrugged. "I'm only creased," he said. "The fall hurt worse than the bullet."

"Are you fit to ride?"

"I can manage."

"Take the Sheriff's horse, then," said Father. "Travel nights, hole up during the day till you are well clear of the Territory. I will give it out that you are dead, and Charlie and I will make a grave for you back along the roadway. I doubt anyone will want to trouble to dig you up and lynch your corpse."

Mr. Grey's laugh was bitter and cold. "Don't be too sure, Mr. Prescott. There are those who would find it a satisfaction."

"Where will you go?"

"North. Into Canada. A lot of my people went that way before the War. It strikes me as good a place to start over."

Mr. Grey came over to me and stood looking down into my tear-stained face.

"Charlie," he said, "it is no good saying I am sorry. You have lost a great friend, and 'sorry' can't bring him back, or ease the hurt, or make things right between us. But I want you to know that I am proud of you—for a lot of reasons. I would like to shake your hand and part friendly."

I couldn't speak, but I did put out my hand. He took it in both of his and squeezed it hard. "God bless you, Charlie Prescott," he said. "I won't forget you, ever."

"Is there anything you would want me to say to Susannah?" Father said.

"Show her my grave," said Josiah Grey. And he touched his heels to his horse and disappeared into the darkness that shrouded the Wind River Range.

EPILOGUE

I have been a long time away from Wyoming. But yesterday a letter came, a letter in a dear familiar hand still firm despite the passing years, bidding "her boy" come home.

Clara, I will come. And after we have had our talk, and dried our tears, I will walk out to where my father lies—and Mother, too, and Jamie and Sheriff Finn—to say a prayer, to lay fresh flowers on their graves.

And I will ride out to that grave, the unmarked empty monument to a friendship that forever altered the direction of my life—a friendship tried and shaken, but stronger now for weathering the shifting winds and changing seasons of a life I'd gladly live again.

I am coming, Clara. I have been too long away.